W9-AYR-957

Pretty Boy Hustlerz
Part 2
Victor L. Martin

Wahida Clark Presents Publishing

60 Evergreen Place

Suite 904A

East Orange, New Jersey 07018

1(866)-910-6920

www.wclarkpublishing.com

Library of Congress Cataloging-In-Publication Data:

Victor L. Martin

Pretty Boy Hustlerz Part 2

ISBN 13-digit 978-1947732-04-9 (paper)

ISBN 10-digit 9781947732049 (paper)

ISBN 9781947732056 (hardback)

ISBN 9781947732070 (ebook)

ISBN 9781947732070 (audiobook)

LCCN: 2017913684

1. North Carolina- 3. Drug Trafficking- 4. African American-Fiction- 5. Urban Fiction- 6. Prison Life

Cover design and layout by Nuance Art, LLC

Book design by NuanceArt@aCreativeNuance.com

Edited by Linda Wilson

Proofreader Rosalind Hamilton

Printed in USA

Also by Victor L. Martin

Nude Awakening III: XXX-Rated

Pretty Boy Hustlerz 1 & 2

Nude Awakening II: Still Nude

Motive For Murder

Nude Awakening

The Game of Deception

For the Strength of You

Unique's Ending

Menage's Way

A Hood Legend

Anthologies

What's Really Hood?!

(with Wahida Clark, Bonta, Shawn "Jihad" Trump,
and LaShonda Teague)

Even Sinners Still Have Souls

(with Darrell King, Tysha, and Michel Moore)

Dedication

RMW AKA Goldie = Wiz Khalifa & Charlie Puth
"See You Again"

- Acknowledgments -
Victor L. Martin

All praise to God for blessing me with this talent to write. Yet again I sit here in this prison cell, writing a new shout out for a book. This is an act that I'll never take for granted. I'll begin with a major shout out to my boss, Wahida Clark. I don't have enough room on the page to express the love & respect I have for you. Thank you for everything. I can't forget the editors with WCP. Because of y'all, you've made me a stronger writer and I am humble to work with each and every one of you. To my super group of friends that support me, Renita M. Walker, Jolene Paige, Yolanda Patterson, Kim Allen (my 1st typist), Anne McArthur-Burt, Desiree King, Patt McGee, Angie Moore, Felicia Moore, Chanail Paree, Tamika Razz, April D. Torain, Jennifer Willis (#1 fan). And with a new twist, I'll mention a few of my readers that support me on my Facebook page, Lissha Sadler, Saphia Inspire, Nahkila Butler, Rek Lvnlife Price, Nicole Alford-Pollard, Shawnetta Marie, Robert Marsh, Author LaToya Copher, Candice Murdock, Lynette Robinson, Richard Aswanu, Adrienne Overstreet, Tonya Wilson, Author Carlene Bowman, Donna Gatewood, Stacey K. Parker, Dell Banks, Lakeysha Reese, Jenny Jet, Kisha Green, Twandra Williams, Silk White, Joyce Veronica Burton-Harper, Vanessa Rodriguez, Jean Henson-

James, Kim Temple-Walker, Christial Inthlord Love, Latasha Williams, Ghason Davis, Tabeitha Pollard Mann, Marie Guammami Santiago, Delon Anoshi Hagood, Mizzdoubleg Ny'Jalea, Lamar Patterson, Barbara Grovner, Lisha Foster & IamStephanie Denise, thank you all for your support because without you there is no Author Victor L. Martin. And to sick with my custom to name a few of my readers behind bars with me, D. Williamson aka Fresh, Trap Money from East Spencer, Eric Dunn, Ashley Parks, Derrick Foreman aka Big Juss, Unique, Dice, Roberto Sanchez, Justin Graham, and how could I ever forget Perry Joines aka Black and a special mention to his sis, Joanne Joines aka Sweet P. A big thanks to my team of typist, Isaiah David Paul, Allyson M. Deese, Antwon Will Coxe, Claire Duncan and Jennifer Jimminez. And I must mention my fellow authors that are *write* behind bars, Ca$h, Kwame Teague aka Dutch, and Darrell DeBrew. And over the years the following authors have reached out to me, Joylynn M. Ross, J. M. Benjamin, Rumont TeKay, Leo Sullivan, T. Styles and Carl Weber. BTW, to all of my fans that enjoyed *Nude Awakening 1 & 2*, guess what's coming, *Nude Awakening 3*! And in closing, a special mention to my mom. It's all about you & I love & miss you so much. To my sisters, Angie & Tremika, my niece Janayla, my nephews Dominique, Ty Riq, and (RIP) Ty Kilo. The countdown to my homecoming is short. I'm humble in what I do and it's without an ego. To all of my readers, thank you for your support and until next time…Keep your eyes dry & Your heart easy.

Theme song for this book: De La Soul "Stakes is High"

P. S. I'll go ahead and put myself on front street and make a statement. When it comes to penning sex scenes, from here on out I'll let my writing show why I've earned the moniker aka Mr. Sex Scene. And if things pan out, I'll be teaming up with the lovely BBW Porn Actress Farrah Foxx #NudeAwakening3! And to all my haters. Just know that I'm like the dark side of the moon to y'all. You can't see me & that's not being on an ego trip, just stating the facts. And shouts out to Selma, N. C. and my old hood down in Liberty City (Miami, Florida). I will return.

-Author Victor L. Martin

(Continued from Pretty Boy Hustlerz: Part 1)

Chapter Seventeen

Maury Correctional Institutional 2:25 a. m.

"I can't wait to have you hard and in my mouth," Sergeant Parker told Mac in a seductive tone.

"Hopefully, we can work that out when you come back to work," Mac whispered back to her.

He gained her full trust and knew she wouldn't flip when he told her about his cell phone. Mac instructed her to cop a new prepaid card cell phone so he could call her. With him being able to talk to her more freely without anyone around, it strengthened the bond they had.

"Please be safe with that phone," she warned for the hundredth time.

"What I tell you about worry about that?"

"I can't help it, Mac."

Mac was lying back on his bunk with a blind over the cell door window. Prison was never meant to be comfortable, but Mac was sure as hell close to it. Things were serious between Mac and Karen Parker after that night she drained him with

5

her lips. The next night he had penned her a one-page letter. Mac wanted her to himself. She bit on his every word, pledging her loyalty and special attention only to him.

"Why you up so late?" He turned to his side.

"'Cause it's the only time I can really talk to you."

"Where your husband?"

"At a bar or something, I guess. I'm glad he's gone, and I wish you were here with me."

"And you know I would be all up in that pussy!" He felt his dick harden.

"You really want to have sex with me? I've thought about it so much, and it gets me so hot that I can't stand it."

"Karen, you already know the answer to that. I want that pussy bad," he replied honestly.

"You're making me wet," she moaned. "Please send me another video of you jacking off."

"I gotcha, baby. But I'd rather let it build up, so I can have a big load for you if we can get some alone time."

"I like that idea now that you said it."

"I figured you would. But um, I still want that video of you fucking yourself with that black dildo."

"Mmmm, so you like how my pussy look?"

Mac rolled his eyes. "I love it and I can't wait to lick it," he lied. Well, it wasn't a lie because he would break her off with some tongue for his own personal gain. Each time they spoke on the jack, he was learning more about her and what lines she would and wouldn't cross. He would be patient with her and not fuck up a good thing. Mac heard of some inmates bagging a female CO, then flip on some blackmail bullshit, fucking the game up. Mac had no rap for fools that couldn't think their way out of a knee-high maze.

"Mmm, that sounds nice. And maybe I can let you have your way with me."

"And which way is that?" Mac asked.

"Anyway, you like. Just know that I'm for real about this."

Rule #1 is important when dealing with a female CO, never be the first to ask for a favor. Mac knew if Karen had the heart to bring him *anything* she would do it on her time and terms. Being that he hadn't asked her for a pack of gum, it pushed her to be more inclined to do favors for him.

"What's on your mind?" he asked setting the tone that it wasn't all about phone sex or texting x-rated words for pussy shots. Dealing with a female guard as opposed to a woman on the street required a different approach.

Karen sighed. "You," she replied. "It's crazy how fast I grew feelings for you, Mac. I will *never* open up to another inmate like I have with you. You just don't understand how stressed out I am, but with you, I have so much to smile about."

"That goes both ways, Karen."

7

"Uh, I have to tell you something, but please don't get mad at me okay?"

Mac sighed because when people mostly said that, bullshit was soon to follow. "What's up?"

"I… um, had an affair behind my husband's back. And… well… see it was last year at the Christmas party at my job. Okay, I had a lot to drink and I was loaded. And… um… I snuck off to a back room and had sex with another guy and he was sorta drunk too, I guess."

"Ai'ight. But I don't see why I would get mad, Karen."

"I… the guy works here."

Mac didn't know what to say. CO's fucking CO's wasn't a big deal but the information caught Mac off guard. *Damn! I wonder who the fuck it was?* "Did your husband find out about it?" Mac paused for a moment.

"No. But like I told you it happened when I was drinking."

"So, you still got something going on with this dude?"

"It's hard to explain, Mac."

"Do you feel like talking about it? If not… I can understand, okay."

"Are you mad at me?"

"No, Karen. But it sounds like you're letting it stress you out."

She sighed, turning quiet. Something was indeed stressing her out. Her complete trust wasn't firm toward Mac just yet.

She badly wanted the chance to confide in Mac, even with a pessimistic view that he could help her.

"Are you okay?" Mac asked, breaking the mold of silence. "Why you getting all quiet on me?"

"Sorry... just had something on my mind. Oh, I checked on that info you needed and the PERT might come next month."

PERT was the Prison Emergency Response Team. They were supposedly a team of specialty trained guards that were called in to go head to head with an inmate uprising. In reality, the PERT were usually seen twice a year during a full institutional lockdown to conduct a search for contraband. The inmates always had a heads up on the so-called surprise visit from the PERT. But as always, a motherfucker would get caught slipping and get sent to lockup for their carelessness.

"Do you want me to hold your phone when they come?"

"You'd do that for me?"

"Of course, Mac. I don't want to see you in the hole. Even worse, you'll be gone for six months. Plus they might ship you to another prison."

"You gonna gimme my joint back, ain'tcha?" he kidded.

She laughed. "You already know what I *really* want to give you."

"Mmm... I forgot. So remind me right quick."

"I want to give you some of this hot stuff between my legs, Mac."

"Nah, I don't want some... I want *all* of it."

"I love it when you speak like that."

"Where you at?"

"In my bed. And I'm on my back with my legs open... and I'm rubbing what I want to give you, Mac," she moaned. "Ahhh... I want your big, black cock all up in my pink hold. Will you stick it in my pussy, Mac? Mmmm, I really need it right now... I need your cock sliding in and out of me hard and fast. Real fast and from the back."

"Lemme hear how wet that sweet pussy is." Mac slipped a hand under his boxers. Closing his eyes, he squeezed his dick with the sloshing pops from Karen fingering herself teasing his ears. Phone sex soon followed when Mac grabbed a tube of A&D ointment off his desk. He had the excitation of jacking his dick honed to an art. Most nights he did it with the aid of viewing a fuck flick on his smartphone. He could go all night long watching Pinky or Cherokee D'Ass getting fucked. Tonight it was all about Karen. He wondered how it would feel to be inside here. Mac stroked his dick at a speedy pace while Karen moaned and gasped in his ear.

"Mmmm, dats my pussy ain't it?!"

"Yesss!" she replied in a throaty tone "It's your hot pussy. All yours and my—"

"Block hot! Man making rounds on the bottom low side!" a voice sounded in the block.

Mac jerked up off the bed and bolted to the door. The cold smooth cement floor chilled his bare feet. "Hold on, baby," he whispered. "Lemme call you back after the block is clear." He ended the call, yanked the towel down, then jumped back on the bunk and slipped under the covers.

When the CO strolled past his cell, Mac appeared to be knocked out. Not a second after someone shouted the block was clear, Mac was up out of the bed putting the blind back up. On the down low, Mac knew the same routine went down with four other guys in A-block that were on-line. Mac already told Karen that he had to end all calls anytime the block was hot. In most cases, there wasn't time to say goodbye. Once he was back on his bunk, he called her back and she answered after the first ring.

"Ai'ight I'm back," Mac called out as a toilet was flushed in a nearby cell.

"Everything all right?"

"Yeah. That was Bladey making rounds."

"I'm surprised he's not asleep in the booth. Okay, where were we?"

Mac swiped his touchscreen to pull up a fuck flick. He muted the hardcore porn that showed an old film featuring Heather Hunter. "I was hoping to make you cum tonight. Are you ready for it?"

Karen replied then started touching herself. Mac's focus was on the screen of his smartphone. It took Karen almost five minutes before she reached her climax.

"Wow, that was good, Mac." Karen was out of breath. "Did you cum, too?"

"You know I did," he lied, searching for a new film featuring MILF's, *Mothers I Like to Fuck.*

"Mac, when we have sex, do you want to cum inside me?"

"Do you want me to?" he turned the question back on her.

"I've been thinking about it. Really, all I think about is finding a way for us to do it, Mac. It's like... such a strong urge, and I can't get it out of my mind. Like I told you that last time we talked, I loved having you in my mouth and doing it that one time. I just don't know what to say."

"Your actions are speaking loud enough for me, so it's all good."

"Mac, why did you kiss me that night?"

"'Cause I wanted to, and to show you how I'm feeling you."

"Funny how my own husband doesn't even kiss me like you did."

"That's because we're two different people."

She sighed. "Mac, don't take what I'm about to say the wrong way. But I can't believe I'm doing this with you. I guess we really can't control what a heart wants."

"And what does your heart want?"

"To be… wanted. I was under a ton of stress before we hooked up."

Mac turned to his side toward the wall, pulling the sheets and blanket up over his head. The time on the touchscreen showed 2:48 a. m. "Stress ain't good for nobody."

"I know, honey. Hey, do you smoke? I can bring you a pack if you want me too."

"Let's hold off on that 'cause I don't wanna see you being fired over a pack of smokes," Mac whispered. He didn't want to appear thirsty for her to start bringing him items in on the low. In his first letter he wrote:

I just wanna get to know you on a personal level at your speed and on your terms. I'm not out to make you no mule. All I want to do is to keep a smile on your face. And if the chance is given, I'd like to return that special favor you did to me. Above all, we need to build a bond of 100% trust between the two of us and trust must be earned. You're the only female I'm dealing with and I have no reason to lie to you. Let today be the start of something special.

P.S. Rip and flush this when done

xoxo

Your Secret

That same night she had written him back, slipping the words under his door with a sick call form.

My Secret

I can still taste the flavor of your sweet dick in my mouth. Tonight was special to me and I'm sure you enjoyed what I did to you. I regret nothing. Sure it's odd and I know what we're doing and have done is wrong, but I don't care. Well, I do, but it doesn't change how I feel about you. I want that trust you spoke of, let's earn it together ok.

Mac read it twice before ripping it to pieces and sending it down the toilet.

"Now it's my turn to tell you not to worry about me getting fired. I can get you a pack if you want one, Mac. I know a little bit about how things go on in the blocks. I'd rather give you your own pack than for you to buy it from someone in there at an outlandish price."

Mac knew the hook was set. All he had to do was sit back and reel her ass right on in. "I'm good, baby. You ain't gotta bring me nothing in but your smile and um… that hot pussy you've been promising me."

14

"Aww, Mac. You're too good to me." She warmed by his words. "But I need you to trust me when I tell you it won't be a problem. I can get it in if I want to. And another thing, I changed my mind."

"About what?"

"I need your help, Mac. I told you most of my stress is from my husband and how my marriage is falling apart. Well, someone else is under my skin and I'm starting to feel trapped."

"Who is it?"

Karen took a deep breath then released it slowly. "Dixon," she told him. "He's the guy that I had sex with at the party."

Mac felt like he was being played by Dixon. In truth, the sudden twinge of raw jealousy surprised him. He wanted to know why Dixon had made it know of his affair with Hart but not a word about Parker? Mac got up on some emotional shit and told Karen not to stress her issue because he had her back. The question stood as to how far he would go in keeping his word.

Chapter Eighteen

Lorenzo and Travis were back on the road after leaving the strip club. Derrick led the way in his Charger until they had made one short stop at a gas station in Princeton. Lorenzo stayed inside the XTS while Travis and Derrick spoke with three new guys standing around a forest green 300.

"So who are those dudes behind us in the 300?" Lorenzo asked when the three sedans neared the city limits of Goldsboro.

"The rest of the PBH crew. The driver is Choppa and the heavyset guy is Jeremy and the white guy is Justin."

Lorenzo nodded. "So how does this shit suppose to go down? If it ain't but one person that needs to be dealt with, why is it taking six of us?"

Travis sighed. "You just have to trust me on this."

"That isn't the point. I don't know jack about your cousin nor them jokers behind us. What if something goes wrong or—"

"Ain't shit going wrong, bruh. Just chill and stop stressing yourself out. All of this will be over soon."

The PBH crew ended up at an upscale subdivision of brick homes about half a mile from the hospital. They all slowed to a stop and turned their headlights off. Lorenzo realized the games were over when Travis reached in the back and grabbed two ski masks.

***

At the same time, thirty-nine-year-old Toni Kenzel was prepared for another night of infidelity behind her husband's back. She stood in the kitchen in a pair of red pumps and a matching satin kimono. The guilt that tugged at her heart and mind would be covered with the drinks she was fixing. A bottle of Zarco tequila would set her mood just right. Behind her, the sofa in the living room was pushed up against the wall. In the new space, three thick solid black quilted bed sheets were lying out on the floor. All around the large dimly lit living room were several lit scented Chanel Number 5 perfume candles. Toni poured her second glass of tequila, and then she strolled toward the living room. The Kimono hugged her soft curves, and she trembled each time the fabric teased her pointy nipples. Getting comfortable on the floor, she tried to think about the pleasure she was about to experience with two men. Nervously, she sipped her drink, glancing at her watch and then at the front door. She had no worry of her husband of eight years coming home tonight. He was an Air Force pilot currently on a six month deployment in South Korea. Her two kids were with her sister tonight so Toni could let loose in her sexual needs. When her watch showed 3:10 a. m. there was a knock at the door. Loosening the top of the kimono, she looked down at the heavy line of cleavage now exposed. Her light brown voluptuous breasts swayed with her steps as she neared the door. She knew her looks were in order from her long hair to her gold painted toenails. The porch light remained off on purpose when she answered the door. "Hello, baby," Toni purred as Jeremy stepped inside and closed the door behind him.

"Damn. You look so fine!" Jeremy rubbed his hands on Toni's ass. "Sorry, I'm a little late."

She kissed him briefly on the lips with her arms around his neck. "It's not a big deal. But, uh, where is your friend?" she glanced curiously at the door.

"Waiting in the car. I just want to make sure you're still okay with doing a threesome. So are you? If not, it can just be the two of us."

Toni smiled. "I haven't changed my mind."

"I see we'll be doing it in the living room." Jeremy got excited.

"And in the kitchen too if you're up to it." She rubbed his chest.

Toni and Jeremy had met five months ago at the Department of Corrections Shooting range in Smithfield. Their common bond was based on their jobs working for the state. Toni was the internal affairs officer at Eastern Correctional while Jeremy worked as a CO at Bertie Correctional. Their bond quickly crossed the line to sex after

Toni began to complain of her bland sex life with her husband. Jeremy had no qualms to fuck with Toni on the down low. Fucking with Toni was both pleasure and business with Jeremy. Each time he was with her he would seek inside details on what was going on at Eastern. Her position had her in the mix of everything. Three weeks ago they were in bed and she told him about a new investigation that could advance her career. Even though Jeremy dicked her down on the regular he knew she couldn't be trusted with any information on PBH. That door was now wide open when he learned she was getting information on Justin who worked at Eastern. Jeremy knew things would get hot when he told the others about what he had learned. Ever since then, Jeremy had to play it safe around Toni.

"Are you still working on that big investigation on that drug ring at Eastern?"

Toni frowned. "Let's save any talk about my work for later. I have bigger things on my mind," she said and then she reached down to grab his erection under his jeans. "But since you asked, I'll be submitting my preliminary report to the superintendent next week."

Jeremy nodded.

"What's wrong, baby? Why don't you look happy? If you don't want me to do this threesome, I'll understand Jeremy."

"I just had something on my mind." He forced a smile. "Let's get started before my friend thinks we're bullshitting."

"I want to take care of you first before you bring him in."
Toni got excited about tonight.

They undressed slowly in the living room, showing patience in their moment of lust. Once they were naked, Jeremy took control of things.

"Sit on my face, baby. Lemme taste you while you do me."

Toni shivered when she got down on all fours on top of Jeremy. A low moan eased through her lips when Jeremy flicked his tongue between the fold of her pussy.

"Yesss!" she moaned. Closing her eyes, she moved her hips in a lazy circular spin. When she heard him slurping and smacking between her thighs, she sang out his name in a chant. Shuddering, she lowered her lips to kiss his balls. Showing no regrets, she grabbed his hard throbbing growth and started sucking on it up and down. She was familiar with his needs, so she made it a point to suck slowly while rubbing his balls. For three straight minutes, her slurps and humming sounded around his wet dick filling her mouth. She wanted to continue, but tonight was meant for more.

"I'm ready," she shivered with his dick against her face. Before Jeremy could reply, she eased her lips back down the length of him. She stayed on his face, sucking the hell out of his dick even as he made a phone call.

***

Lorenzo entered the candle lit living room two minutes later with a box of condoms. Travis told him his part was simple. *All I have to do is fuck this chic and pretend I'm a friend of Jeremy's,* Lorenzo thought, as Jeremy made the quick introductions between him and Toni. After that, Lorenzo was told to remove his clothes and shoes. At first, he hesitated until Toni and Jeremy started the fun without him. Toni went down on all fours again taking it from the back. Her large breasts swung like a pendulum beneath her as Jeremy pulled her long hair back while smacking her bouncy ass. Toni shrieked each time Jeremy slammed his curved dick deep inside her spasmodic pussy. When Lorenzo finally joined them, she stared up at him for a moment, then focused her attention on his erection. Aroused pass the point of self-control, she eased Lorenzo inside her mouth, tenderly wrapping her lips around his long shaft.

Toni couldn't believe the raw power she had over both men. At one point she was riding Lorenzo while jacking Jeremy's dick. Then she was on her back with her ankles up on Jeremy's shoulders. He pounded her hard and fast for six straight minutes until switching out for Lorenzo. They took turns inside Toni in the living room for an hour and a half straight. The smell of sex floated thick and strong. The bottle of Zarco was empty, and Lorenzo had used all three condoms. Toni couldn't stop herself from tasting Lorenzo at the kitchen table. His cum had a different taste than Jeremy's, and she wanted to swallow him again before Jeremy finished with his shower. Midway through her act, she had a second idea.

"Can you do me from the back right quick?" Toni asked from her knees between Lorenzo's legs.

"I'm out of condoms."

"It's fine with me without one. My tubes are tied and between us," she licked up the length of his dick and then swirled her tongue twice around the tip, "I like having you inside me over Jeremy."

Lorenzo couldn't side with using the head on his shoulder. Toni was too succulent to turn down. Rising from the chair, he bent Toni over the table and then he eased his spit slicken erection between her pouty pussy lips.

"Oooohh shit!" Toni gripped the edge of the table as Lorenzo gave her his full length with each thrust. He held a firm grip on her by the waist as his steady strokes sent her wide ass bouncing back and forth. She humped backward against his strokes with her face on the table. In and out he drilled between her thick thighs, making her pussy fart and pop around his thrusts.

The session in the kitchen lasted seven minutes. Toni urged Lorenzo to stay inside her when he reached his climax by rolling her ass against him. Reality hit Lorenzo when he filled Toni with his cream. He was drained and upset with himself. *What the fuck am I doing here! I need to be home with my family, not up in here fucking this dumb ass bitch.*

Toni stayed bent over the table while Lorenzo pulled his penis out of her grippy hole.

"That was a nice piece of work you just did. If you can keep a secret, how would you like to hook up some other time? Just the two of us?" Toni offered with a satisfied grin.

Before Lorenzo could turn her down, there was a sound at the front door. Toni frowned.

"You uh, expecting anyone?" Lorenzo asked as Toni picked the kimono up off the floor.

"No. But wait here while I see who it is."

Lorenzo was pulling up his boxers when Jeremy walked into the kitchen.

"Take a seat, Toni," Jeremy blocked her path.

Toni tied the kimono around her waist and then she stared at Jeremy. "I need to see who is at the—"

"Sit the fuck down!" Jeremy shouted.

Toni took a step back. She assumed Jeremy felt some type of way over her solo actions with Lorenzo. "If you can't speak to me like you have some damn sense I suggest you—"

Jeremy hauled back and punched Toni in the face, sending her flat on her ass. She howled in pain with blood trickling from her nose and busted lip.

"Man, what the fuck you hit her for!" Lorenzo ran up on Jeremy as Toni curled up in a ball behind him on the floor.

"Man, you better get the hell outta my grill before yo' ass be on the floor wit' that bitch!" Jeremy sneered.

"Try it and see what will happen!"

"Both of y'all need to chill." Travis suddenly stepped up behind Jeremy and placed a hand on his shoulder.

Lorenzo flexed his jaws to let Jeremy know he was upset. "This fool up in here tripping!"

Travis stood next to Jeremy with Derrick, Justin, and Choppa behind them. "Relax, bruh."

"Relax!" Lorenzo shouted. "Look at what he did to her face!"

Toni cursed when she saw Justin. "What the hell is this? I want you all out of my house this second!" she shouted.

"Tie the bitch up," Derrick said just as Toni made a dash for the phone.

Her screams filled the kitchen as Jeremy, Choppa, and Justin wrestled her to the floor.

"What the fuck!" Lorenzo tried to rush to her aid but was held back by Derrick and Travis.

"Chill man!" Travis ordered as Toni started to cry.

"Get the fuck off me! I Ain't down for this bullshit just—"

"The bitch is the internal affairs officer!" Derrick shouted in Lorenzo's face.

Lorenzo's jaw dropped. "What?"

"Go in the living room and get dressed." Travis released his grip off of Lorenzo's arm.

"Please help me, Lorenzo!" Toni cried from the floor beneath Jeremy, Choppa, and Justin.

"Why didn't you tell me who she was before I fucked her!?" Lorenzo jerked away from Travis, then stared at Derrick. "And the bitch knows my fucking name!"

"What does it matter?" Derrick shrugged with a smug look on his face. "She gave up the pussy, so be happy."

"What are you going to do with her?" Lorenzo directed his question at Travis.

"Change of plans," Travis replied.

Toni had a bad feeling, mainly due to the sight of Justin. She knew her problem was linked to her current investigation surrounding Justin and his drug ring at Eastern. Sobbing non-stop, she pleaded for them to leave, offering them anything they wanted. Jeremy showed her no sympathy when he tied her to the kitchen chair with a black extension cord. Her heart pounded with fear when she was left alone with Jeremy and Justin.

"Tell me everything you know about Justin and the Pretty Boy Hustlers," Jeremy commanded as he stood to Toni's left.

Justin stood across the kitchen leaning against the stove with his arms crossed.

"Why are you doing this to me?" she cried.

Jeremy sighed and then pulled a stainless steel snub-nosed .38 from his waist, then placed it against Toni's head. She broke down in a wave of tears that were ignored by Jeremy.

"Tell me everything you know about PBH, Toni. This can end either good or bad for you. The choice is yours. Now answer my motherfucking question!"

Chapter Nineteen

Goldsboro, North Carolina 4:50 a. m.

"All we're gonna do is ask the bitch a few questions and scare her up a little bit," Travis explained to Lorenzo in the living room.

"This some bullshit!" Lorenzo shouted as he paced back and forth. "You should've told me who the fuck she was before I fucking did what I did. And what if this stunt doesn't scare her? She knows my name and face!" Lorenzo threw his arms in the air.

"The bitch ain't gonna say nothing," Derrick tried to convince Lorenzo. He could tell Lorenzo wanted to flip.

"Ain't asked you shit!" Lorenzo turned toward Derrick. "Seriously, bruh. It's best not to say another fucking word to me!"

"Y'all need to chill fo' real!" Travis glared at them both. "We in this shit now, so it is what it is. So deal with it!"

"I'm getting the fuck up out of here!" Lorenzo started for the door but stopped halfway. *I can't leave her like this.* "Who's running the show here?" Lorenzo asked Derrick and Travis. "Is it that punk ass Jeremy in the kitchen?"

Derrick laughed. "Zo, you ain't going nowhere, and it's none of your business who is calling the shots."

"Yo, Travis. You need to put your fam up on game real quick-like because he's fucking with the wrong one!" Lorenzo stated.

"For the last time! Both of y'all need to motherfuckin' chill!" Travis stepped between Lorenzo and Derrick. "I'm calling the shots, so there it is! Derrick, go in the kitchen while I talk to Lorenzo for a minute."

Derrick grilled Lorenzo hard before he turned and headed for the kitchen. If it was made known, Derrick hated being told what to do. For now, he would let the drama with Lorenzo slide since Travis was in the mix.

***

Toni had no other option but to tell Jeremy and the others the truth. With blood crusted around her nose and lips, she explained how Justin's name ended up on her desk. A fellow officer on Justin's shift had grown suspicious of Justin being too friendly with a certain inmate. Toni further explained her next moves of watching the frequent interactions on camera between Justin and the inmate. After three weeks of investigation, she had gathered enough evidence to place Justin under notice of an investigation.

"Who else have you told about this?" Jeremy asked as he stood over Toni.

"No one," she mumbled with her head down. "I needed to be sure Justin wasn't working alone with what he was doing."

28

"Have you spoken to the inmate?"

Toni closed her eyes. Giving up wouldn't do her any good. As long as she kept talking she stayed alive. "Yes. I talked to him a few days ago. I told him about my knowledge of Justin smuggling in drugs and contraband. He tried to deny everything," she opened her eyes and then she stared at Justin. "He broke down easily and then he told me everything."

"And you're proud of that, huh?" Jeremy yanked her chin up and then he shoved her face. "Where is the full report that you plan to show to your boss?"

"On my computer."

Jeremy nodded at Justin and then glanced at Derrick to see if he had anything to add. Derrick stayed quiet as Justin walked up to Toni and held out a small picture. Toni's heart sunk at the sight of her two kids playing at the park.

"Here's the deal," Jeremy looked Toni in the eyes. "Of course, we were never here. But you are gonna do me a big favor. When you go back to work I need that file and any paperwork on Jeremy to go away. Do you understand what I'm saying? Because if you do anything other than that, I'll kill both your kids and I'll do it in front of you. Are we clear?"

"I'll do it!" Toni cried. All she cared about were her kids. She wouldn't attempt any type of plan to contact the police. She would do what was demanded and nothing more.

Jeremy remained silent for a brief moment. "Our little affair can continue if you're ok with it." He traced the outline of her left breast with the .38.

"We're not here for that bullshit!" Travis stated as he entered the kitchen.

Jeremy lowered the .38. "Bitch ain't worth fuck anyway."

"Where Lorenzo?" Derrick asked Travis.

"Using the bathroom. Yo, so y'all got everything in order up in here?" Travis glanced at everyone.

Derrick nodded. "Yeah. But are you sure we can trust this bitch won't run to the police?"

Travis pulled a chair from the table, then sat down in front of Toni.

"I'm not going to the police," she sobbed.

"What's more important to you? Your job or your kids?" Travis asked Toni. "The choice is up to you."

"My kids! Please trust me. I promise I'll do it," Toni pleaded with Travis.

"Do you know who I am?" Travis asked.

Toni lowered her chin. "No."

"If you do what we're asking you to do, you'll never see me again and it's just that simple."

Toni didn't know what else she could do or say to prove her cooperation with their demands. Keeping a clear mind to stay alive was her main focus. A second fear of being raped was growing from the hard stare she received from Justin. Above all, she just wanted them to leave so she could call to check on her kids.

Travis glanced over his shoulder at the others. "You got anything to say, Justin? All of this bullshit is because of you not knowing how to move in silence!"

Justin shook his head. "Nah. I know I screwed up."

"Damn right you did!" Travis shouted then slid a hand down his face to regain his composure. Sighing, he turned back to Toni with a flat expression. A second before he opened his mouth to speak, Lorenzo barged into the kitchen.

"Fucking police outside!" Lorenzo shouted.

Travis shot to his feet as Justin and Choppa hurried to the kitchen window. "How the fuck! Yo, Jeremy, check the—"

"We need to get missing, cuzzo!" Derrick stated. "And I mean like right now!"

As panic filled the kitchen, Derrick eased a black .380 from his back pocket, then nodded at Travis. The next span of events was left up to Travis' quick decision. Thinking that all was lost, Travis returned the nod to his cousin just as Jeremy aimed his .38 at Toni's forehead.

***

Goldsboro police officers Randy Perrillo and Scott Santos responded to a tip on a robbery in progress. Both were alert

31

and suspicious of the call since the dispatcher said the tip came in anonymous.

"What's the ETA on our backup?" Santos asked from the passenger seat.

"Too long for us to wait," Perrillo replied as he slowed to a stop in front of Toni's home. "I'll go up to the door. I want you to cover me from the driveway, okay?" Perrillo instructed.

Santos nodded. "Just be careful, man. I have a weird feeling about this."

Perrillo turned the emergency lights on, and then he made a quick report back to the dispatcher.

A minute later, Perrillo carefully made his way up to the front door. Out the corner of his vision, he saw Santos in position with the pump action tactical shotgun. The strap was unhooked over Perrillo's holstered 9-millimeter pistol. Easing up to the door, Perrillo became tense because it was too quiet. Just as Perrillo prepared to knock, a string of gunshots sounded from within the house. Perrillo instinctively drew his weapon and ducked below the darker windows. Behind him, Santas called in a new report of shots being fired.

***

Lorenzo stumbled to his hands and knees as Travis shoved him through the back door. The second Lorenzo stood on his feet he took off running in Toni's back yard. Lorenzo ran toward a waist-high chain-link fence and jumped it with ease.

"We gotta get back to my car!" Travis blurted as he ran next to Lorenzo. Lorenzo ducked under a clothesline that nearly took his head off. He wanted to know who was shot and why. But now was not the time to be holding a discussion. Jumping over a second fence the two came out on a new street behind Toni's home. Travis pointed to the left and then he took off running as the steady tone of police sirens grew louder. Running at full speed they hauled ass up the block then cut a path across the front yard of a large two-storied home. A set of lawn lights blinked on in their wake. The police sirens seemed to come from two directions. Both were out of breath when they reached the XTS.

"We gotta get the fuck out of here now!" Lorenzo said as he closed the door.

"Chill, bruh! We good." Travis' hand shook as he reached up to adjust the rearview mirror. Derrick's Charger sat a few yards behind him.

"Who got shot?" Lorenzo asked.

"I don't know."

"Man! This shit is all fucked up! Why are we just sitting here?"

"I'm not leaving my cousin."

"What if he was shot?"

"He wasn't shot, okay?"

33

"How the hell you know?" Lorenzo asked. "You just said you didn't know. What if the police caught him? We can't just sit here and wait all fucking night!" Lorenzo stared at Travis. "We need to get the fuck up out of here, Travis!"

"I'm not leaving!" Travis started the engine but left the lights off. "We have to wait. The police ain't looking for us."

"How do you know!"

"I just fuckin' know, okay!"

Lorenzo punched the dash, then slumped back into the seat. "This some bullshit!"

***

Derrick slowed to a stop to catch his breath. Sirens sounded behind him, but he was well hidden beside a parked van. Breathing heavily, he pulled out his cell phone to make a call.

"Fam, where the fuck you at?" Travis asked after the first ring.

"Two blocks from you! Yo, listen to me. I got a spare key stuck under the front bumper on the right. Come and get me 'cause I can't make it to you."

"What happen back—"

"I'll explain it later! We need to bounce before the police block us in."

"Where you at?"

"Ah, I'm at the corner of Martin and Wilkerson Street."

"Alright, fam I'm coming. Just hold tight!"

Travis nor Derrick spoke a word until they were back on the highway.

"Did you do it?" Travis switched lanes with the high beams on.

"I don't trust your boy back there," Derrick pointed over his shoulder at the pair of headlights.

"Answer my fucking question! Shit, if it wasn't for Lorenzo we would've never gotten away!" Travis stated.

Derrick sighed. "Yeah I did it! But I still don't think we should've left that bitch alive."

"She won't go to the police."

"And you're gonna bet your freedom on it? The bitch got three dead bodies in her kitchen man! This shit is all fucked up and it was your stupid ass idea!" Derrick shouted.

"Oh, it's stupid now?"

"Gotdamn right it is! We should of killed that bitch and you know it!"

"Then what about her file? She's the only one that can erase it! She saw how real this shit is. She don't know us so the threat about her kids is still real to her," Travis explained.

"Too many holds, man. Too much can go wrong and I don't like it. And don't let me get started on your idea to go in without our masks." Derrick stared at Travis. "I'm not understanding shit you're doing fam. Ain't no way I'm going down for any of this bullshit!"

"It's gonna work out. All we need to do is play our role and chill. We got too much invested in PBH to let it fall. Trust me. Ain't nothing gonna go wrong."

Back in Goldsboro, Toni rocked back and forth on the sofa with tears slowly rolling down her face. She appeared to be in shock, but in truth, she had to get her facts in order. Around her, a crime scene unit moved around the living room and in the kitchen behind her. Whatever lie she told, she had to stick with it. She cleared her throat and then she motioned to the head detective that she was ready to give her statement.

She admitted that she knew Justin since it would eventually be discovered. "He works at Eastern Correctional."

"And what's your connection with him?" the detective asked.

"We were having an affair," she lied.

"What about the other two men?"

"I never saw them before."

"Okay. Now, can you tell me what happened here tonight?"

Toni nodded yes. "Justin came over and we had sex. He... left the door open for the other two and they slipped in and caught us off guard."

"Us?"

"Yes. Justin had it set up like a robbery that he wasn't a part of. The big guy in the black jeans, he hit me when they came in and I acted like I was knocked out. While I was on the floor in the kitchen I heard them arguing."

"About what?"

"The other two. They wanted to rape me, but Justin was against it. After I was tied to the chair, they kept going at it, you know. Justin became upset when he realized I knew he was teamed up with the other two. Next, someone yelled about the police being outside and that's when the shooting started. I had my eyes closed and they just shot it out and killed each other and I don't know why."

Chapter Twenty

Wilson, North Carolina

July 25th, Thursday

One month later.

"I want to make a toast," Travis announced up in VIP at Club Twerk It. Seated with him were Lorenzo and Derrick. At midnight, the VIP was jumping.

"A toast to what?" Derrick asked with his elbows on the table.

"PBH nigga! And to all the bread we putting in. Just the three of us." Travis nudged Lorenzo with a grin. "Shit is running just like I told y'all it would."

"I can't argue with that." Derrick sat back then cocked his head toward Lorenzo. "Why you so quiet tonight? Heard you made that power move at Eastern like it wasn't nothing."

Lorenzo shrugged then lifted his glass of Hypnotiq to his lips.

Travis chuckled. "Just give him some time to get adjusted to things."

"I see you got a new ride." Derrick crossed his arms. "'Bout time you got rid of that hit up Accord."

Lorenzo stared across the table at Derrick. "Why the fuck you worried about what I drive?"

"Whoa!" Travis stood. "Y'all need to dead this little beef right fucking now! Matter of fact lets settle this right now so what's up?"

Derrick sucked his teeth. "I'm good. I was just fucking with him. But I see he can't take no jokes."

Travis sat back down. "We came here to discuss business. Not beef with each other over no dumb shit. Now about our numbers, we have a new market to supply and the demand is high."

Lorenzo paid close attention to Travis speaking on a new hustle behind bars. Prescription drugs, and the lick would focus on Oxycodone. The money was the hook that had the new PBH chain draped around Lorenzo's neck. Travis explained how he was planning a nighttime robbery of a major pharmacy in Havelock, North Carolina.

"We'll come away with nearly 30,000 ten milligrams Oxycodone. And here's the good part. The police, mainly the DEA, will be expecting the pills to hit the streets. But we all know where we'll sell every single pill." Travis grinned.

"Behind bars," Lorenzo answered as he stole anther quick glance at the time.

Travis lifted his glass. "Now how about we make a toast? PBH forever!"

Lorenzo and Derrick pushed their beef aside to make the toast with Travis. Their glasses clinked above the table. With the mood at peace, Travis slid the curtains back to wave three strippers over.

Lorenzo slid back in the seat as a thick redbone stripper sat down on his lap. She had most of her titties exposed in a tiny bikini top. *This can't be her real hair.* Lorenzo thought as the girl flipped the blonde mane over her bare shoulder. Her thick frame enticed Lorenzo. But Lorenzo was anxious to leave.

Next to Lorenzo, Travis whispered in the ear of a tall, dark-skinned stripper with extension braids down to her ass. She giggled at whatever he said then sat up to pull her tank top off. The third stripper was the hazel-eyed cutie, La'Ashia. Lorenzo couldn't take his eyes off her.

"Can I talk to you in private, Derrick?" La'Ashia stood with one hand on her small waist. "Now," she pressed, looking upset.

Derrick sighed as he eyed La'Ashia up and down. Tonight she had her body laced in a backless, pink bustier and a matching pair of ass hugging, tight boy shorts. Not wanting to start a scene, he got up from the table to see what the fuck she wanted.

"I'll be back in a minute." Derrick nodded at Travis then reluctantly followed La'Ashia out of VIP and down to the first-floor lounge.

"I see you're enjoying giving me your ass to kiss!" La'Ashia called out when she sat across from Derrick at a small table near the back exit.

"How the fuck you gonna say that when you're the one that changed your phone number and shit!" Derrick stated. "Ain't 'bout to be letting you stress me out over no dumb shit. I thought I made that clear after our last issue."

La'Ashia frowned. "It was more than just an issue, Derrick. How the fuck you gonna call yourself being in a relationship with me when your ass was fucking another bitch behind my back!"

"That was after I heard about you leaving the club with some dude from Raleigh!"

"And I told your ass that nothing happened!" she snapped.

Derrick sighed as La'Ashia glared at him with her arms crossed. "What do you want from me?"

"How about a bit of respect? I know our relationship was bumpy. But you don't have to throw it in my face by ignoring me and being all up on these other bitches up in here like I don't see it!"

"I was coming to the club before I met you."

"That's a dumb excuse, Derrick."

"It ain't an excuse. It's the truth."

La'Ashia fumed and thought of the night she caught Derrick up in VIP fucking Creame. She and a few other strippers knew about Creame's side hustle because it was an in-house favor by a few others. La'Ashia knew Creame would hustle Derrick for a 'sex for money' trade and it was La'Ashia that made the video and then sent it to Shaun. She hated seeing him with other girls in the club after their five-month on-and-off relationship had failed.

"If I give you my new number will you call me?" she asked after a quick glance at the PBH piece around his neck. Derrick sat back in the chair with a smug expression. He couldn't live with La'Ashia but fucking her fine ass was a different story. With her favorable looks toward Christina Milian and a high sex drive, he enjoyed her company and porn star quality sex. "And what would we talk about?"

La'Ashia cleared her throat. "For starters. We can talk about starting over and take it from there."

"What if I want to see you tonight?"

She forced a smile. "I guess it would depend on what you're trying to see."

Derrick lowered his eyes to the tops of her breast pushed up in the pink bustier. It was pointless to try to fight his attraction to her. "What if I want to see everything?"

La'Ashia finger a loose strand of hair out of her face. "That might can happen. But you're not taking me to a motel."

"You saying you wanna come home with me?"

She knew pussy filled his thoughts by the way his eyes took in the sight of her cleavage. Sticking with the motive she nodded yes.

"How do I know you ain't trying to bullshit me?" Derrick asked straight-faced.

La'Ashia slid back from the table, then pointed at the pussy print under her tight boy shorts. "Because she needs some dick tonight."

Derrick motioned her to come and sit her pretty little ass on his lap. He inhaled the strawberry scent between her soft breast when she circled her arms around his neck. In the dim lit space, he slid his hand between her thighs and rubbed her softly. "I got all the dick it needs," he said, sliding his other hand up and down her back.

"I was hoping you would say that. Um, give me ten minutes to clean out my locker, and I'll meet you back here." La'Ashia swished her tongue inside his mouth as he nodded yes.

***

The time, 2:50 a. m. showed on the dashboard inside Lorenzo's brand new royal blue Ford Explorer sitting on chrome 24's. He left the strip club thirty minutes ago, and now he sat inside his SUV parked at a motel in Kinston. Sighing, he adjusted the black and chrome Ruger 9 millimeter on his lap. *What the fuck have I gotten myself into? This isn't the life I want.* Lorenzo would give up his new SUV, the easy money, and all ties to PBH in a heartbeat if it could reunite him with Shayla. Things between them were all the way fucked up since

43

Mikki answered his phone. Last week he finally got to the truth on how Shayla found out about his cheating ways. Mikki came clean and told Lorenzo about answering his phone, but she left out the part that Travis played. With Shayla on his mind, he picked up his cell phone but couldn't find the courage to make the call. Seeing an unread text message from Kahneko, it laid a ton of guilt on his shoulders. He couldn't find any fault in Kahneko, and if it weren't for his feelings toward Shayla, he could see himself spending more time with Kahneko.

Five minutes later, he sat up in the seat when Mikki's Infiniti Q60 pulled into the parking lot. Lorenzo flashed his headlights, then reached across the center console to grab his smartphone and the room key. Tucking the gun in the front of his jeans, he hurried across the unlit parking lot and met Mikki at the room they would share. She smiled at him as he gave her a hug. "Sorry I'm late." She nervously glanced around the parking lot as Lorenzo unlocked the room.

"What held you up?"

"I have to look my best for you." She brushed up against his arm.

Mikki had on a pair of black skinny jeans that squeezed her thighs, ass, and hips. Her voluptuous breasts were enhanced by the white V-neck blouse that displayed all of her cleavage. Just to be cute, her hair was tied in a ponytail with two strands hanging past her cheeks.

"Are you sure we have to do it like this?" Lorenzo asked as Mikki lowered her purse on the bed.

"You having second thoughts?" Mikki waited for his answer before she took off her blouse and bra.

"Nah. It's just… well, we already did a threesome, so why would Kahneko trip about us fucking?" He shrugged.

Mikki unbuttoned her blouse while she stepped out of her Manolo Blahnik heels. "That was only a one time affair, baby."

"So now we have to creep on the low behind her back and Travis?"

Mikki nodded yes as she folded her blouse. "Can you deal with that? Don't get me wrong, Kahneko is my girl and I'm feeling Travis. But when it comes to my sexual needs…." She walked up to Lorenzo and turned around so he could unfasten her bra.

"What about 'em?" Lorenzo removed her white lacy bra then tossed it on the bed.

"I'll do whatever to cater to my needs." She closed her eyes when Lorenzo reached around her to cup both of her tits. "Can this be our secret?"

Lorenzo filled his hands with her breasts. "It's cool with me."

"I have an idea!" Mikki looked over her shoulder. "Do you have to work tomorrow night?"

45

"Yeah. Why? What's up?"

"I was hoping we could spend the weekend together," she cooed, pressing her ass against his hardness. "Let's just lay up and fuck and have fun."

"Don't worry. I'll break you off real proper like."

"I don't doubt it, baby," she said as his hands continued to fondle her breasts. "You've already shown me how you can work my middle.

Lorenzo turned Mikki around and lowered his mouth to her nutmeg toned nipple.

"I've been waiting for this moment," Mikki whispered as her nipple throbbed between Lorenzo's lips as she closed her eyes and reached between his legs to massage the lump under his jeans. "I really couldn't have my way with you when we did that threesome last month. And I didn't get the chance to finish you off." She shuddered.

Lorenzo circled his tongue around her nipple with no care for his actions behind Travis' back. One on one with Mikki excited Lorenzo, and tonight he hoped she would act on all the freaky shit she'd been blowing in his ear over the phone. They both showed patience when they kissed at the foot of the small bed. Item by item they stripped naked until their clothes pilled around their feet.

"Mmm, I want you to fuck me so bad, Lorenzo!" Mikki moaned as she caressed the stiff flesh between his legs. She shuddered again as his tongue slid up the space between her titties and his hands squeezing her ass. "Do me!"

Mikki's raspy voice was laced with lust and need. Lorenzo willed himself to think of the moment and not of Shayla. Minutes later Mikki helped him achieve that goal by licking and kissing her way down his nude frame. He pushed his fingers through her fine hair as her lips and tongue teased the tip and sides of his erect penis. For the next several minutes she sucked gently on his flesh until her name stuttered through his lips. When she pulled her wet mouth from his dick, she licked it three times to savor the flavor of his clear gel.

"You enjoy that?" Mikki rose to her feet.

Lorenzo managed a nod, wanting nothing more than to be balls deep between Mikki's warm thighs. He took the submissive role and allowed her to straddle him on the firm bed. Mikki licked his neck while grinding and writhing her pussy over his strong erection. She lightly bit his ear as she reached behind her to guide all of Lorenzo between her wet folds. They both moaned when he entered her.

"Yes!" Mikki gasped and wasted no time to feel more of him. Her body rocked back and forth, forcing his iron to ease in and out at the pace and depth she wanted. "Squeeze my ass!" she moaned in his ear. "Ohh! This feels so fucking good!"

The bed squeaked when a slow, steady pace was discovered between them. Their moans became a chorus of heavy breathing, mixing with those wet slurping sounds below their waist. When she sat up on him she whimpered while bouncing up and down on him. Her breasts heaved with her movements that went on and on as her ass clapped against his body. He encouraged her to take his dick. At times, he would smack her quivering ass or palm both of her mouth watering breasts. He warned her of his sudden rush toward his release. She kept bouncing and swirling her wetness all over his dick. Her powerful sex caused Lorenzo to pull at the cheap bed sheets as Mikki rode him through the peak and end of his climax.

"Spend the night with me," Mikki later suggested in the dark room as she rested her head on Lorenzo's chest.

"Don't you have to check in with Travis? What if he calls you over?" Lorenzo asked.

Mikki rolled her eyes. "Travis don't own me, Lorenzo. And if he was to call me, I wouldn't answer his call. I'm with the man I want to be with tonight. And I hope you can show me the same favor if Kahneko was to call you.

He smiled. "Yeah. I can do that. So, how did you hook up with Travis?"

She sighed. "Baby, you're going to spoil the mood."

"Okay. You have a point. What do you want to talk about?" Lorenzo slid his hand under the sheets to rub her warm ass. Mikki licked his nipple and then she snuggled closer against him.

48

"Umm, let me suck you off right quick. And after that, how about you tell me how you earned your PBH chain."

Chapter Twenty One

Selma, North Carolina

July 26th, Friday

"Tell me the truth and don't lie to me," Michelle hounded Shayla the second she stepped inside her apartment.

"Truth about what?" Shayla frowned as Michelle took her green sunglasses off.

"Don't act like you don't know what I'm talking about." Michelle dropped her Fendi tote bag on the sofa. "I'm staying with you this weekend and you're gonna tell me the truth."

Shayla couldn't meet Michelle's stare as she sat down on the sofa. "How are things down in Miami?"

"Fine." Michelle stayed on her feet. "I found a nice house in the same spot as Trevon and

Kandi. Now answer my question." Michelle waited for an answer.

Shayla knew she was busted. "About what?"

Michelle sighed and rolled her eyes. "When you were down in Miami with me last month. Who came to the hotel room while I was at the beach?"

"Trevon. He, um, came by to drop the script off to you."

"And why did you lie and tell me it was somebody else?" Michelle crossed her arm as a wide grin eased on Shayla's

51

face. "I knew it!" Michelle threw up her arms in the air. "You and Trevon did it that night, didn't you?"

Shayla couldn't hold her secret in. Coming clean she told Michelle about her chance encounter with Trevon that single night. "I didn't regret doing it." Shayla smiled. "We talked about porn of course and he kept telling me how sexy I was. It was wild. One minute we were kicking it on the sofa and the next minute we were all over each other. And he was so big and hard!" Shayla crossed her legs as a short spasm throbbed between her legs.

"I want details," Michelle demanded.

"We did it. I fucked him, okay," Shayla replied. "Actually, we did it twice!"

"You are *sooo* bad!" Michelle laughed as she gave Shayla a high-five. "Now, I'm not worried about you getting mad at what I'm about to tell you."

"Don't bet on it," Shayla responded.

Michelle shocked Shayla by telling her how she had arranged the visit by Trevon. Shayla had made her fantasy thoughts of Trevon a reality last month down in Miami. In a sober state of mind, she used her hurt over Lorenzo to give herself to Trevon. It was a one-night stand she would never forget.

"I figured you wouldn't mind since you talked about how bad you wanted to meet him," Michelle told Shayla her reason for her actions. "Was it good?"

"Yeah." Shayla refused to give up the details of her one-night stand with Trevon.

"Did you go down on him?"

"I won't answer that." Shayla giggled. "What I did with Trevon will stay between the two of us and you're not included."

Michelle rolled her eyes again.

"What's up with you and your new gig, Miss Porn Star."

"It's good. I'll start my first film next week with Trevon and another girl."

"A threesome?"

"Yep. The title will be *Cookie and Creame* and it will be filmed on a boat."

"I still can't believe you're a real porn star!"

Michelle shrugged, "It's what I want to do. Um, you still stripping at Twerk It?"

"Only on the weekends."

"I wouldn't mind going with you tonight. I bet Shaun would be surprised to see me. What is Sayveon up to?"

"Nothing much. Still working VIP and the main floor on the nights I'm there."

"He's a weird man if you didn't know. He feels that oral sex doesn't count towards being unfaithful."

"That's TMI." Shayla didn't care how Sayveon viewed what cheating was or wasn't.

"Oh, is Derrick still tossing his money away up in VIP like a fool?"

Shayla shrugged. "I haven't seen him since that night I first met him," she lied with a straight face.

"That's a surprise because his ass be up in the club 24/7. But anyway, I plan to tie a few things up before I go back to Miami. I really appreciate you letting me stay with you."

"It's not every day I can open my crib up to a famous porn star," Shayla kidded as Michelle blushed.

"Gimme a year and *then* I'll be famous!"

Shayla was happy for Michelle and she let it be known by promising to be her biggest supporter. She chatted with Michelle on the subject of her new life down in Miami. Michelle surprised Shayla with the 411 on a new boyfriend that owned four high-end car lots down in Miami.

"And he's cool with you doing porn?" Shayla had trouble understanding how an open relationship could work.

"It's really our common ground because he's a former porn star." Michelle reached inside her tote bag and pulled out her cell phone. "Here's a picture of him."

Shayla waited as Michelle swiped her finger across the screen. When Michelle smacked her lips at a certain picture Shayla asked who it was.

"My deadbeat baby daddy! I have to go to court later today to file child support on his ass. I don't need his money but he has to face some type of responsibility for his son."

"He gotta job?"

"Yeah. He works at a prison."

"You never told me anything about him."

"That's because I just did a DNA test on him last month. He wasn't my man or nothing like that. The only reason I still have his picture in my phone is to show it to my son one day. I hate it has to be like this but I'll learn from my mistakes."

"What's his name?"

"Travis Dixon."

Shayla gasped. "Travis Dixon from Greenville?"

"You know him?" Michelle looked up from her cell phone.

"Let me see his picture!" Shayla jumped up off the sofa and took a close look at the clear picture on Michelle's cell phone. "I'll be damn! That's him with his Drake-looking ass! You got a baby by Travis."

"How do you know him?"

"He's like a brother to my baby daddy."

"One that you never told me about."

"That's because I don't deal with him no more. But wow! You and Travis and his sorry ass never told me nor Lorenzo about having a baby."

"He ain't shit! The last time I spoke to him I tried to be cordial but she showed his ass. All I wanted was for him to be a park of Rikeith's life. I don't need his money nor his dick."

Shayla sat beside her friend. "I have a plan. Do you want to see him face to face?"

Michelle pondered the idea for a brief moment. "Sure, why not."

***

"Ooohhh, Derrick, please don't stop!" La'Ashia moaned beneath Derrick with her legs hooked over his arms. She gasped and fought to control her racing breaths as he fucked her.

"Dis that good dick, ain't it?" Derrick spoke through his clenched teeth with the light on.

"Yesss!" she replied, covered in a sheen of sweat. For the second night in a row, Derrick took full advantage of the opportunity to go between La'Ashia's legs. He moved with quick strokes that kept the headboard thumping against the wall. Stroke by stroke he pushed hard into her wetness as her fingernails clawed his sweaty back. His bedroom reeked of used condoms and rough sweaty sex. CLAP, CLAP, CLAP, CLAP, were the unremitting sounds of their bodies crashing flesh to flesh. La'Ashia dug her fingernails into his skin each time he tunneled balls deep insider her. Her throaty moans matched the speed and depth of his demanding strokes that curled her pedicured toes. Rough sex at its best stood in favor to La'Ashia. She knew the firm difference between her needs and her wants. Tonight she needed to stay focus on the scheme of things and not the pleasurable firm object that distended her slippery folds. In and out it reached deep, driving La'Ashia wild and with wantoning lust. Catching Derrick off guard, La'Ashia reached between their bodies and lightly moved her fingertips under his balls. Derrick raced between her legs, pounding and driving himself to a knotted stomach climax. La'Ashia massaged his balls and kissed him hard as the throes of his climax subsided. He licked her nipples hungrily.

"Mmm, that was good!" La'Ashia admitted as Derrick eased himself out and rolled from between her sweaty legs. "And we did it for, like, forty minutes straight this time!"

"We got one or two more condoms left." Derrick wiped the beads of sweat from his forehead. "Damn, I forgot how good your pussy was," he laughed.

La'Ashia rolled to her side, reaching between his legs to removed the ribbed-sided condom. The task was the norm for her and she did it while swirling her tongue in his ear. With the condom removed and dropped in the trash, La'Ashia leaned up and smiled down at Derrick.

"What time is it?" he rubbed his fingers up and down the soft space between her slippery breasts.

She leaned over him, mashing her titties on the side of his face as she looked at the screen of her smartphone on the nightstand. "Five minutes to ten."

"Shit! We've been in bed all day."

"Is that a problem, baby?" She rubbed his stomach, knowing her touch would result in a new growth below his waist.

"Hell no." He grinned. "You got me wanting to put that pussy under lock and key."

"Good." She kissed him on the lips. "I'm kinda feeling we can get things on the right track between us. For all it's worth, I missed you like crazy, Derrick and I seriously mean that. We both did our wrongs in the past and it's behind us now. Do you feel the same?"

He nodded as she raked her fingernails down his washboard stomach. "You don't have to leave tonight."

She grinned. "Is that coming from your heart? Or this?" she took his soft penis in her hand and played with it.

Derrick's stomach sunk from the sudden deep breath he took. "You trying to wear me out?"

"Perhaps," she giggled. "But tonight I'd like to show you what you've been missing. Let's take a nice cozy bath by candlelight until we can do it some more."

***

58

"What's that smell coming from the kitchen?" Derrick slid his hand up under his shirt that La'Ashia had on.

"I'm warming your steak up."

Derrick caressed her bare ass then worked his fingers between her legs. "Mmm... pussy still a little damp." Smiling at her from the tub he removed his hand and patted her lightly on her ass.

"Maybe I'll let you lick it after you eat."

Derrick smiled. "Ain't no maybe to it."

Shaking her head she sashayed on her bare feet out of the bathroom. "Rest up because I want a lot more of that dick." She moved past the kitchen and ended up back in Derrick's bedroom. Moving with a set purpose, she rushed up to the black and brass mirrored drawer to scoop up her cell phone. *I know his stash spot is up in here somewhere!* She started her search inside his walk-in closet. *Nigga got more shoes than me.* Holding her cell phone out at arm's length she snapped a picture of the closet. A timer ran on the phone on the top right corner of the screen. She had only three minutes to find what she knew was under his roof. A look under the bed seemed pointless. With two spots to check, she started with a large trunk at the foot of the bed.

"Damn!" she whispered. It was locked. Moving back toward the dresser she assumed he had some type of stash spot hidden behind one of the nine drawers. Just as she reached for the top drawer she noticed a deep imprint on the tan carpet along the base of the dresser. La'Ashia took a step back and saw the meaning. The dresser had been slid forward and its weight had pressed the carpet down. Judging by the size of the solid dresser, La'Ashia knew she wouldn't move it an inch. With seconds left she wedged the cell phone between the back of the dresser and took a picture.

"Bingo!" She grinned when she viewed the picture. Turning the screen sideways she could make out the black iron door of a safe build into the wall behind the dresser. Next, she typed a quick text message and then she sent it off.

Found his stash spot. Behind the dresser in his bedroom. TTYL.

La'Ashia deleted the picture and the text before she hurried to the kitchen.

***

Mac and Sergeant Parker did their best to keep their link hidden from Dixon. It was up to Mac to pick which path to travel. Things with Dixon were still running smooth, but with Parker, the sex became an item Mac couldn't pass up. Parker informed Mac that she knew about Dixon and his hustle behind bars. She trusted Mac enough to also tell him how Dixon was using her to get drugs and cell phones inside the prison. Parker's sister-in-law worked in the gatehouse, and it was only on her shift when Parker would bring in the drop.

"He's blackmailing me," Parker had told Mac weeks ago. She went on to explain how Dixon had a sex tape of her in a hotel room. "All it shows is me giving oral sex to Dixon. I didn't know he was filming it, and he kept his face out of the camera."

Mac sat in the sergeant's office with Parker a little after midnight. Time was short so they got to the point.

"Have you thought about it?" Parker asked with high hopes that Mac would help her.

Mac sighed. "What if something goes wrong?"

"It won't. Look, I know, Dixon is making a ton of money, and he isn't giving me a dime. We can take him out of the picture, and then I can bring everything to you."

Mac stared at Parker as he weighed his options. He had not told her the truth about his dealings with Dixon. For all she knew, she assumed he was sprung off her attention and sex. Mac knew his money would triple with Dixon on the sidelines. Parker had promised Mac that his decision to help her would be worth his time and effort.

"When are you trying to make this happen?" Mac asked.

"As soon as possible."

"And what about that sex tape?"

Parker smiled as she slid a sheet of paper across the desk. "I did it last week."

Mac knew Parker was serious. "You… filed for a divorce?"

"Yes. So Dixon can shove that tape up his ass! I'm not afraid of him anymore. So will you help me?"

"I'm down." Mac made his decision then left the office a few minutes later. Heading back to his cell he nodded at Dixon and Hart up in the control booth.

"How is Watson doing at Eastern?" Hart asked Dixon as he popped the block door for Mac.

"Ok, I guess," Dixon murmured as he crossed his arms.

"You've been real quiet tonight. Something wrong?"

Dixon stared at Mac walking inside the block and up to his room. I need a favor," he replied.

"Huh?"

"I need you to write Mac up for a 3-6."

Hart frowned. "Are you serious? Why would you want me to lie on that boy like that?"

"I can't explain it right now. But I really need you to do it for me."

"I'm not feeling that."

Dixon stood up and pulled out his wallet. "Here! Take this." Dixon waited as Hart eye the $100 bill in his hand. "Just write him up and the money is yours."

"Don't ask me to do this again." With no guilt, she took the money.

Chapter Twenty-Two

Kinston, North Carolina

July 27th, Saturday

A little after 10:00 a. m., Travis paid Derrick a visit at his fenced in three bedroom brick home.

"This better be important," Derrick told Travis when they were seated at the kitchen table. Derrick hadn't bothered to get dressed, opting to stay in a pair of shorts and a tank top.

"It is." Travis glanced over his shoulder. "Where La'Ashia?"

"Taking a shower."

"You hooking back up with her?" Travis laid his cell phone on the table.

Derrick nodded. "Something like that. Now what's the problem you got?"

"I think my plug is on some bullshit."

"Mac? I thought you said he was solid."

"I know what I said and at the time he was. Right now he's been fucking with Sergeant Parker too hard."

"How?"

"I think they got something going on behind my back. The fact of Mac keeping it from me ain't sitting good with me."

"You speak to him about it?"

"Nah. Right now I'm just sitting back and watching."

"Parker still doing what she's supposed to be doing?"

Travis said yes then went on to explain the recent funny actions by both Parker and Mac. Travis had noticed how Mac and Parker were finding ways to be alone. One night two weeks ago he swore to Derrick that he saw Parker slipping in the back fire escape area with Mac. As Derrick took in Travis' words, he made a quick assumption that Mac was just fucking Parker.

"It's more than that. Shit, if that was the case I wouldn't give a fuck about it," Travis mentioned as Derrick yawned.

"Just call 'im and see what's up. You're gonna need Mac to move these pills you told me about."

"He can be replaced! Just like you did with Jeremy and the other two clowns. We don't *need* no fucking body to make this bread. I got fifty other hungry inmates lined up behind Mac to take his spot."

"I still think you should holler at him before you cut him out."

"Too late."

"Fuck you mean too late? My money is tied up with your moves at Maury, so how you gonna—"

"I don't trust Mac no more! Simple as that! This ain't like the issue we had when you took Jeremy, Justin, and Choppa out of the picture!" Travis stated with a hard glare.

"That was different!" Derrick shouted. "Them fools had too much heat on PBH and you know it!"

"And yet you did what you did!" Travis matched Derrick's tone.

"What's done is done. What you need to be worried about is that bitch at Eastern. How you so sure she gonna stay quiet?"

"Lorenzo has her under control. If she was going to talk to the police she would've done so by now."

"I still don't trust that bama!"

"Man, you need to dead that bullshit because Lorenzo is solid."

"Yeah and you said the same about your boy Mac, too."

"What's up fam? You feeling some type of bad vibes on Lorenzo or are you just hating on him?"

Derrick pounded the table with his fist. "Look at what the fuck you're doing! You done gave Lorenzo an entire spot at Eastern and he hasn't put in no type of work for PBH! So what he's cool! This is business, cuzzo!"

"Tell me now I'm fucking up?" Travis' eyes blazed. "Do I need to point out who picked Justin to work at Eastern? I told you he wasn't ready to hold that spot down and look what happened."

Derrick slid his hand down his face. "Look man, and listen to me. I got a bad feeling about Lorenzo so I'ma put it out there."

"But why?" Travis looked confused. "Dude putting in work."

"Think back to that night in Goldsboro. Remember how he was on that captain save a hoe for that chick Toni?"

Travis grinned. "He was pussy whipped."

"I'm serious, man! Remember we were all in the kitchen and—"

"He went to use the bathroom so what?"

Derrick sighed in his frustration of Travis missing the point. "I think your boy Lorenzo called the police that night."

"Get the fuck outta here." Travis shook his head. "Why would he do that and risk going to jail?"

"He did it to save that bitch! I bet he thought we were gonna murder her ass. Think about it, fam. We bust in without no mask and rough the bitch up. Lorenzo ain't got no loyalty to PBH. He ain't built like us."

"That might be true. But I still don't see him calling the police. And... even if he did, we can never prove it."

"We can't move forward with that nigga in doubt fam. If he called the police his ass needs to be dealt with. Just because y'all are buddy buddy doesn't give him a free pass!"

Travis couldn't force himself to admit Derrick's words made sense. "All we'll be doing is assuming shit."

"Not really. I know how we can let 'im tell us on his own."

"How?"

"By his actions. A guilty dog will bark."

"And you have a plan for this?"

"Of course I do. And I'm telling you now. If your boy is sour he's a dead man and it's not up for a debate."

As Derrick explained his scheme to Travis his words were being secretly recorded by La'Ashia. She stood hidden around the corner wall in the living room getting more dirt on Derrick and Travis. Five minutes later Travis slid back from the table to go and use the bathroom. By the time he strolled into the living room, La'Ashia had dipped back to the bathroom at the end of the hall. When she heard Travis in the guest bathroom she breathed a sigh of relief.

Back in the kitchen, Derrick stood at the kitchen sink looking out the window at Travis' XTS. Too much loot stood at risk and Derrick wasn't ready to let anyone stop his hustle. His crib, his name brand gear, and rimmed up Charger was linked to PBH. As he turned, Travis' cell phone chimed on the table. When he neared the table he got a big surprise of the picture caller ID filling the screen.

"What the fuck?" Derrick picked the cell phone up and started at Shayla aka Monàe. *How the hell these two know each other?* Thinking nothing of it, he answered the call and changed the tone of his voice just a little. "Hello?"

"Travis?"

"Uh, he busy right now. Can I take a message?" Derrick had fallen back from Shayla a few days after the drama in Goldsboro. The two had met up for a date in Raleigh, but the night didn't end in Derrick's favor. To be blunt, Shayla didn't give up any pussy.

"What time will he be able to talk? I really need to speak to him."

"I'm not sure. Just try back in a few minutes. He should—"

"Who the hell you talking to?" Travis walked up behind Derrick with his hand out for his phone.

"Some chick," Derrick mouthed as Travis took the phone. He stared at Travis and tried to read his reaction to seeing Shayla's picture and number on the screen.

"Hey, Shayla! What's up?" Travis sat back down at the table as Derrick stood behind him leaning against the sink.

"Nothing much, who was that answering your phone?"

"My silly ass cousin. Lemme guess, he tried to holla atcha?"

"Nah."

"So, you calling for Lorenzo?"

"Nope. And I don't want to hear nothing about him. I called because I heard something about you that I hope isn't true."

"I'm listening."

"Why are you dissing my girl, Michelle?"

"Who told you about her?" Travis stayed calm.

"She did. And yeah it's a small world. FYI, I read the paternity test results so it's no need to deny your son."

Travis sighed. "How long you've known about this?"

"Since yesterday. Now, what's up with you? She said she tried to talk to you but you were on some other shit."

"She with you now?"

"Maybe. If she is, will you man up and talk to her? Y'all don't need to drag this out in the courtroom."

Travis didn't need any issues with Michelle. "Yeah I'll talk to 'er."

"Good. Now can you meet us at the mall in Goldsboro?"

"What time?"

"Is six good for you?"

"Yeah."

"We'll be at that urban book kiosk and don't be late."

"I won't," Travis answered as Derrick stood over him with his arms crossed. "Do you need me to tell Lorenzo anything when I—"

"Nope. I'll see you later."

Derrick didn't speak until Travis ended the call. "Who was that?"

"You don't know her."

Derrick grinned. "Wanna bet?"

"Yeah I'll bet."

"Shorty a stripper."

"Wrong." Travis stood.

"Wrong my ass! That's Shayla aka Monàe from Selma. She drives a gray Altima and—"

"She told you all that?"

"Fam, I know the chick. I met 'er last month at the strip club."

"Shayla ain't no fucking stripper!"

"I got 'er number in my phone! Why do I have to lie? Shit… you fucking her or what?"

"She's Lorenzo's baby momma."

"Word? So how the fuck she—"

"Hold up! Did you know who she was when you met her?"

"Man, did you hear what I said? I just met the bitch last month and now you're telling me she's Lorenzo's BM!"

"Did… you fuck her?"

Derrick motioned for Travis to lower his voice. "No. But now you can't tell me that nigga Lorenzo, ain't on no grimy shit! You expect me to believe I met ole girl by chance?"

"Relax, fam and let me think about this shit." Travis closed his eyes for a second then snapped his fingers, popping his eyes open. "Did you meet Shayla before or after you met Lorenzo?"

"I met her first."

Travis frowned. "And she was stripping?"

Derrick went ahead and told Travis about the lap dance that jumped off with Shayla. "The bitch is up to something! What did you talk to her about just now and who?" Derrick paused as La'Ashia strolled into the kitchen.

"Hey Travis." she smiled. "You staying for breakfast?"

"Nah, but thanks."

"Lemme see your phone for a sec." Derrick had an idea to remove the doubt from Travis' mind.

"For what?" Travis asked.

"Show La'Ashia ole girl pic and let's hear what she has to say."

"What's going on?" La'Ashia played dumb to what was going on as Travis grabbed his cell phone off the table. A second later her mood flipped as Travis held the screen in her direction.

"How do you know this girl?" Travis asked.

La'Ashia rolled her eyes. "She strips at the club and she's a favorite to your cousin. She calls herself Monàe, or something like that. Umph, you fucking with that tramp, too? Keeping it in the family, huh?"

"I didn't fuck 'er," Derrick stated. "All I had with 'er was that one lap dance and that was it."

"And that better be it!"

"I wonder if Lorenzo knows anything about Shayla stripping?" Travis asked as La'Ashia brushed past Derrick.

"You going to meet that bitch, huh? It's a set-up fool!"

Travis shook his head. "Shut up fool. You don't even know what you're talking about. Shayla isn't on no bullshit like that."

"Oh yeah? Then tell me why you found it so hard to believe her ass was stripping? You don't know the bitch just like you don't know Lorenzo."

Travis hated to admit that Derrick words had a ring of truth.

"I'm telling you that something is up," Derrick added. "You're the one that put Lorenzo down with PBH, so I'll let you correct this shit. I didn't like the bum from day one!"

Travis had to stick with his promise to get up with Shayla and Michelle. With his third eye itching, he asked Derrick to join him for the ride to Goldsboro later on.

"Why she wanna see you so bad?" Derrick asked.

Travis steered Derrick from the truth about Michelle and his son. "She just wants to see if I'll tell her what Lorenzo has been up to, I guess."

Derrick nodded. "Something ain't right, fam. And don't tell me to chill because I know you feel it too. I just hope you know what you're doing."

Chapter Twenty-Three

At the same time back in Kinston, Lorenzo reflected on his actions with Mikki behind Travis' back. For most of Friday, he had a wild marathon of sex with Mikki that tested his stamina and skills in the bed. At the moment, he was alone in the room since Mikki had left for food only minutes ago. Today she promised him more sex after he agreed to spend the weekend with her. He stared at the ceiling, waiting to match her stroke for stroke.

He glanced at his watch; 10:25 a. m. Lorenzo had learned a little more about Mikki during their brief breaks from sex. She opened up to him after he spoke on PBH. He learned that Mikki had met Travis at a club in Greenville two months ago and their bond was based on sex and a little business. The business aspect circled around connections to help Travis get the best grade of weed in Coastal North Carolina. She didn't smoke and like most women she was private of her age. But to tame Lorenzo's curiosity she told him she was in her early thirties and left it at that. Kahneko entered their talks when she sent him a text last night asking him to call her. Mikki spoke fondly of Kahneko and surprised Lorenzo when she mentioned how she met Kahneko the very same night she met Travis. Being they were the only two Asian females in the club, they mingled upon sight and built a new friendship. Lorenzo couldn't stop from asking if Kahneko had ever joined in a threesome with her and Travis. Mikki laughed about it and told Lorenzo she doubted it would ever happen.

She also told Lorenzo that the night he met Kahneko was the first time Kahneko had ever been to Travis' apartment. When he asked why Kahneko had made the trip with her, she smiled and told him it was Travis' last second, asking her to bring a friend for Lorenzo's company. She told him about her home in Havelock and that she stayed a few blocks from Kahneko. As mentioned before, their breaks from sex were brief and Lorenzo had no issues when Mikki had started up her kinky acts under the bed sheets. He stood at the bathroom sink brushing his teeth when Mikki later returned with the food. She sat a bag of men's cosmetic items on the dresser with the food and greeted Lorenzo with a long erotic French-kiss in the middle of the room. They ate and had sex twice on the stained bed sheets. At one point they were going at it hard when Mikki's smartphone started to ring on the night table. By its tone, she knew Travis was calling. She ignored it as Lorenzo ran his dick in and out of her pussy from the back. After nearly an hour and a half of hard-core sex, Mikki wailed out his name as she climaxed around his long throbbing penis. Panting to catch her breath she told him not to move an inch. Minutes after the first-morning taste of Lorenzo she slid from the bed to take a quick, needed shower. To her delight, he joined her and showed his thirst of her lovely breast by sucking each nipple until she moaned in pleasure.

The shower wasn't big enough for them to do what they wanted to do. Mikki halted their attempt after she banged her elbow on the wall. They made use of the shower for its intended purpose and washed each other from head to toe. Mikki got out first after she stroked Lorenzo to his full length with her hand. She left him in that state as her pussy twitched from the sight of him.

"Looks like you got him up and ready again." Lorenzo reached for Mikki's hand as she stepped out of the steamy shower.

She glanced down at his new growth and bit her bottom lip. The urge to have him back inside her made her nipples stiff. "You want some more of me?" she blushed.

Lorenzo turned the shower off and joined Mikki by the sink. He slid his hands down her wet hips. "You're so damn sexy," he whispered. "I can stay inside you all day."

Mikki softly brushed her nipples against his chest. "Prove it," she grinned. "Show me how good this pussy is to you. Fuck me like this is your last taste of it."

Lorenzo acted on his lust toward Mikki in a rush of movements. They kissed and touched each other intimately. He caught her off guard and showed his strength by picking her up and lifting her up to his shoulders. Mikki squealed as she found her balance up on his shoulders. Her head was a few inches from the ceiling but all she cared for was Lorenzo's next move. The fresh musky scent from her pussy drove him wild. The urge to taste her pulled him to slide his tongue up her thin pussy lips. She jerked as his hands grabbed her soft ass and pulled her sweetness closer to his face. He didn't play around with his face game.

"Mmmm! Baby, yesss!" Mikki braced one hand up on the ceiling while palming Lorenzo's head. Travis or no other man had ever treated her to a freak action that she enjoyed more than she did with Lorenzo. Her pussy leaked over his lips and flowed down his face. Her moves bounced off the walls as his tongue slid in and out of her center.

Again their movements moved in a blur when he lowered her to her feet. Dizzy with pleasure, she tongue kissed him, tasting the raw flavor of herself. She wrapped her fingers around his long rod and stroked it. As one, they moved back to the unmade bed. Lorenzo motioned for Mikki to grab a condom off the night table. In a rush, she tore the package open then slid her hands down to cover him up. Lorenzo moaned as she stroked his dick a few times before rolling the condom over his flesh.

"Please fuck me some more!" She bit her bottom lip as she pulled him on top and between her legs. "All of it... mmm gimme all of it, baby! I want to feel your balls on my ass. Yesss! Ohhhh, just fuck me all *day*!"

Lorenzo slid his erection inside her and went balls deep. Her ankles sat high up on his shoulders as Lorenzo bounced his balls off her juicy ass. The sex grew without emotions between the two. Mikki extended his time inside her by squeezing the tip of his dick each time he neared a climax. When she was on top she popped her ass up and down while riding him backward. Her titties jiggled and bounced with her practiced movements. The bed squeaked as Mikki's pleasure produced moans filled the room.

"I love this dick! I love this dick!" she chanted with her slick pussy sucking his dick up and down. Whatever it took to keep his ass in the room she was down for it.

She wailed out his name when she let him hit it from the back. Looking over her shoulder she twirled her pussy around his stabbing meat. Lorenzo ignored the beads of sweat rolling down into his eyes. Mikki's pussy held his dick in a wet suction-like grip. This was one bad chick that seemed perfect in his view. Neither paused a second when Mikki's smartphone started to ring on the night table. By its tone, she knew Travis was calling. Lorenzo continued to pound in and out while palming her dangling tits. After half an hour of hard-core fucking, he reached a nut.

"I have something I need to show you," Mikki later said as Lorenzo came out of the bathroom. "Grab my purse off the dresser."

Lorenzo figured whatever she wanted to show him would be related to sex. When he handed her the heavy purse, he sat at the foot of the bed with the damp motel towel around his waist. Mikki stayed in the nude, knowing her nakedness would keep Lorenzo in the room.

"Can you help me with something?" She sat beside him.

"Like what?"

Mikki opened her purse then lifted out a large clean bag of yellow oblong pills. "Help me sell these Quaaludes."

Lorenzo's eyes bugged. "What the hell are you doing with all these pills?"

"Making money," she replied. "You do your thing at work and this is how I do me."

Lorenzo removed the bag from her lap. "How many pills is this?"

"A thousand. I know they're worth more in prison, but Travis won't let me make any moves with him. I told you last night we can do some business on the side."

Lorenzo wasn't too sure to deal with Mikki on the pills. It was bad enough that he was digging her back out on the down low. "Where did you get these?"

"I have a friend in Newport and that's all I'll say for now," she lied.

"How long have you been doing this?"

"Long enough to know that you'll make more money by working with me than PBH."

"This ain't nothing but—"

"I can get double the amount that Travis is planning to steal from the pharmacy in Havelock. Don't look surprised that I know about it because I'm the one that put him on to it."

"Okay, if that's true, why isn't Travis getting the pills from you instead of stealing them? Why steal thirty thousand when you claim you can touch double?"

"All Travis wants from me is my weed connect and pussy. If I'm making money on his level, he'll see me as a threat. He's the type of dude that's scared of a real woman."

"And I'm different?"

Mikki smiled. "You're not greedy. So yes, you're different."

"How can we hide our business from Travis?"

"Are you going to help me move these pills?"

"I'm still thinking about it. Travis has his faults, but it doesn't feel right to be doing all this shit behind his back."

Mikki nodded. "I understand. But... while you're thinking it over, let me do something that will feel right while you make up your mind." Mikki slid her hand under the towel and wrapped her warm fingers around his dick. With lust in her eyes, she played with it until it stood up straight. "You don't need Travis or Derrick to be your boss. You can be your own king, baby." She injected these words in Lorenzo's mind to fuel his choice to side with her. She stayed on the theme of oral sex by pulling the towel open to taste him.

***

"I'm not stupid!" La'Ashia shouted at Derrick inside his bedroom. "You're going with Travis just so you can see that bitch Monàe! What type of bullshit are you trying to toss on me?"

"For the last time! I'm not fucking Monàe ok!" Derrick grabbed La'Ashia by the wrist. "Look at me, baby. Ain't gotta lie to you about nothing so stop tripping. You're the one under my roof and in my bed and I want to keep it that way."

"I hope so," she pouted. "I stopped stripping for our relationship to work so don't make me look like no fool!"

Derrick kissed her on the lips. "I'm going with Travis to handle some business and I need you to trust me on this."

"What time will you get back?"

"It'll be before ten. You plan to wait up for me?"

"I might," she shrugged. "Just don't force me to come looking for you," she warned with a straight face.

Minutes later, Derrick stood in the driveway next to Travis. "What's the plan?"

"Follow me to the mall in Goldsboro and watch my back. I doubt she's up to anything in a public space but I'll stay on point."

"What about Lorenzo?"

"Let's handle this shit first. And stay in the cut. I don't want Shayla to see you. I'ma try to catch her in a lie and just roll with it."

Derrick nodded then moved around Travis toward La'Ashia's Mercedes–Benz CLA 45. "Let's get this over with."

"I don't think he's going to show up." Michelle couldn't hide her worry as she sat behind the wheel of the white Range Rover Sport rental.

"Are you coming in or not?" Shayla asked from the passenger seat. "I want to be at the kiosk before he gets here. I don't know why you're afraid to see him face to face anyway."

Michelle tugged the hem of the fitted spruce mint green skirt down her thighs. Her fear of seeing Travis face to face was centered more on her feeling embarrassed. How could she expect him to respect her after she gave up the pussy on the first night? "Ok, I'm ready." Michelle figured it was now or never to finally face Travis.

"Wait in the music store until I give you a signal because I need to get something straight with Travis first. Are you okay with that?" Shayla wanted to help Michelle come to peaceful terms with Travis for the sake of their son.

"Sure. But if he shows his ass, I'm leaving," Michelle stated.

"Stop being so pessimistic about everything. Just let things be and remember it's his loss if he doesn't want to be a part of your son's life."

Michelle nodded. She had to stop worrying about Travis' view of her as a person. In truth, being in a relationship with Travis wasn't on her list of options. Sticking with the plan, Michelle headed for the music store with hopes that Travis would show up.

***

Five minutes to six, Shayla stood at the book kiosk with a paperback novel by Kiki Swinson.

"If I ever write a novel, I'll make sure you're on the cover."

Shayla turned when she heard Travis behind her. For the first time, she felt no guilt to admire Travis and his good looks. *Nah. I'll never fuck Lorenzo's best friend.* "Glad you came."

He shrugged. "No need to try to put it off." He scanned the mall. "Where Michelle at?"

"She's here. But I need to talk to you first."

"About Lorenzo?"

Shayla turned to place the novel back on the stock. "No."

"Damn. Y'all really calling it quits?"

"Lorenzo made his choice to be with that other girl. And to be honest, I don't want to talk about him." She turned back around and crossed her arms. "Please tell me you're not turning your back on your son."

Travis sighed. "It ain't like that. I just needed some time to get my mind right. Real talk, I fucked the bitch."

"She has a name, Travis! And that woman is the mother of your son!"

"My bad. But she pops up outta the blue and forced me to take a test and—"

"You're the father. We all know that's a fact but you're the only one that is tripping. You need to man up, Travis!"

Travis didn't have the words to plea his side of the story. It wasn't like he was tricked into fucking Michelle. Those last few moments after the condom popped was all on him. *Fuck! All I had to do was push a few more strokes them pull out.*" Look, just let me sit down and talk with her ok. I'll help her with the baby and—"

"That's sad. You don't even know your own son's name."

Travis lowered his head. "Can I ask you something?"

"What?"

Travis met Shayla's stare without blinking. "How did you meet Michelle?"

"Why?" *Oh shit! I can't tell him the truth. I don't even know if he knows about Michelle stripping.*

"Because I'm trying to figure a few things out."

"Like what?" She shifted nervously.

Travis grinned. *She's hiding something. I got her ass now.* "For starters, why didn't you come to me if you needed money?"

"Who said I needed money?" She frowned.

"Well, you either need some money or you're stripping for the thrill of it."

Shayla's jaw went slack. *OMG! If Travis knows about me stripping, I'm sure Lorenzo knows too! But how?*

Derrick was strolling through the mall when he spotted Michelle inside the music store. *I know that phat ass from a mile away!* Derrick slipped inside the store and snuck up behind Michelle as she browsed through a rack of Hip Hop CDs. "What's up sexy?"

Michelle glanced over her shoulder then turned to face Derrick. "What are you doing here?"

"Shopping for some new kicks," he lied. "What's up with you? Done went MIA on me. I haven't seen you at the—"

"I don't strip anymore."

"My loss, huh?" Derrick smiled, then noticed the nervous looks she made over his shoulder. "Um, you here with your man?" he assumed. "If so I'll fall back."

Michelle wasn't up for a conversation with Derrick today. Everything and everyone dealing with the strip club was all behind her now. She felt stupid for the risk she took by fucking Derrick and few others at the club. *I have to get rid of him before Shayla and Travis come.* "Yeah, I'm here with my boyfriend," she lied with a forced smile.

Derrick cocked his head. "He's a lucky man. Well, I guess I'll catch you later or something."

Michelle merely nodded. "Take care."

Derrick couldn't resist eyeing her curvaceous frame from head to toe. He only fucked her once, but the pussy was worth every dollar. *I bet she's with a lame ass dude that ain't up on her side hustle of selling ass. Shit, I'd pay for it again!* Just before Derrick turned to leave he saw Creame staring at the entrance. He assumed it was her man. To his speechless surprise, he watched his cousin and Shayla coming toward him. Shayla paused in her steps when she locked eyes with Derrick. When the four stood in a circle it was a stunned silence. Michelle grew tired of the bullshit, so she broke to the heart of everything.

"Do I need to take out child support on you, Travis? Or, can we work things out?"Chapter Twenty Four

Maury Correctional Institution 6:15 p. m.

"I swear to you that I wasn't jacking off on Hart!" Mac explained to Karen over the cell phone. "Dixon was up in the booth all night and you know that. Now that I think about it, Dixon has Hart in his circle. Maybe he told her to lie on me."

"Just don't do anything crazy. I'll handle the write-up, and I think you should put that phone up before they kick your door in. Dixon know you have a phone?"

Mac paced like a caged lion inside his cell. "Yeah."

"Do you trust me?"

"That's not up for any debate."

"Okay, let's make the call now. I have a feeling that Dixon is on to us and for some reason he called in sick. Remember, you must get him to mention his job and something that can prove who he is and what he's doing."

"What if he mentions your name and all the shit you're doing for him?"

"Let me worry about that. I won't put you or myself in a predicament that's too tight for us."

Mac peeked past the towel covering his window. The block was clear and under a code-2 count. Life for Mac wasn't easy, but today he had to make a choice. He sorta felt as if he was snitching Dixon out. *Fuck it! He's the police.* "All right, I'll call 'im now. Are you ready?"

"Yes. And you're doing the right thing, Mac."

Derrick stood in the middle of a real-life soap opera watching the facts unfold. Learning the 411 on Michelle, aka Creame, being Travis' baby mom left Derrick at a loss of words. The circle became complete when Michelle and Shayla found out that Travis and Derrick were first cousins. Michelle felt sick upon realizing she had fucked her baby's father cousin. Everyone tried to speak at once.

Michelle could only hope that Derrick hadn't told Travis about their actions up in the VIP booth.

Shayla stood in the same dilemma with the worry of Derrick telling Travis about her actions in VIP as well. To make matters worse, Shayla had to beg Travis to keep his mouth shut about her stripping.

"I thought you don't fuck with Lorenzo. So why do you care if he knows or not?" Travis pointed out.

"That isn't the point!" Shayla argued.

"What about our son?" Michelle asked Travis as Derrick stood to the side with a crooked grin on his face. The entire situation amused him.

Travis held up his hand when the cell phone on his hip chimed. Since it was his business phone he had to answer. "Lemme take this call right quick." Travis quickly excused himself.

"Whatever!" Michelle stormed out of the store with Shayla and Derrick behind her.

Travis snatched the cell phone from his hip. "Yeah!"

"I call at a bad time?" Mac asked. "You got me worried since you didn't come to work tonight."

Travis sighed. "I got some personal shit going on. What's up?"

"Some bullshit. Your girl Mrs. Hart wrote me up on a bullshit jacking charge!"

"Word?" Travis acted surprised.

"I think she got me mixed up with one of the block janitors or something. You were up in the booth with her all night, right?"

"Yeah. Maybe it's a mix-up. I'll call 'er after I get off with you. So what's up?"

"Yo, what's up with those pills? Our main line on red unit is ready to spend eight hundred dollars for the next drop."

"Won't be 'till next month. I have to handle things on my end first before we can start taking orders."

"Ai'ight. But what about those three watch phones? The ones Watson hit me off with were perfect. Can you get the same model in?"

"It shouldn't be a problem. I'll just holla at Watson to see where he copped them from."

"So he's holding it down at Eastern?"

"Like a trooper."

"You find out who'll be taking his spot on y'all shift yet? I hope it's not an asshole because this unit is straight."

"Most likely it will be a chickenhead from operations."

"Well, I do need a small favor. My battery won't hold a charge no more, so if you can, I'll need a new one."

"Just send me a picture of it and all the other info and I'll bring it in on Monday."

"Thanks. And don't forget to call Hart and find out what's really up."

Travis hung up then hurried out of the music store to catch up with Michelle, Shayla, and Derrick.

"Please don't tell Travis about us." Michelle didn't sidestep what was on her mind. "I didn't know you two even knew each other."

"This is a mess!" Shayla lowered her head on her arms at the table she shared with Derrick and Michelle.

"It will stay between the three of us," Derrick promised to Michelle's relief. "This shit is mixed up as it is so I won't add to it."

"Thanks, Derrick." Michelle reached for his hand and gently squeezed it. She played nice because she needed her actions with Derrick to remain in secret.

Shayla lifted her head. "I hope this isn't some type of game!"

"My mind is on the same idea," Derrick fired back. "I met your man last month after I met you at the club. You must be still fucking with him since you're concerned about him knowing about—"

"You don't know shit!" Shayla stated. "Y'all nigga's might've set all this up from the jump!"

"Shayla, we—" Michelle's attempt to calm Shayla didn't work.

"Nah, I need to speak my mind!" Shayla stood. "How do you expect us to believe one fucking word, Derrick? You just told us that you'll keep some grimy shit behind your own cousin's back. So what you did it with Michelle! It is what it is and Travis' only concern should be on his damn son!"

"Shayla, please!" Michelle pulled Shayla back down. "I'm the one that should be upset. Not you. Now can we discuss what's going on without making a scene?"

"Good to see one of y'all got some sense."

"Go to hell!" Shayla sat filled with regret for falling for Derrick's game.

"Who's going to hell?"

Everyone looked up from the table at Travis. When Shayla rolled her eyes it drew a sigh from Travis.

"Michelle, can I talk to you in private?" Travis asked as Derrick pushed back from the table and stood.

"Whatever you have to say to me you better say it now."

"All right. Where's... my son?"

"Do you even know his name?" Michelle blurted.

"I can't remember," Travis admitted. "Look, I know I've gone about this the wrong way and I'm sorry. I came here to get on the same page with you. Not to argue."

Derrick moved around the table until he stood in Travis' face. "I'ma bounce. Take my advice and make peace with ole girl because we have enough bullshit over our head as it is," Derrick muttered under his breath.

"I'll handle it," Travis replied. Or so he hoped as Michelle glanced impatiently at her gold stylish watch.

***

Back at the motel in Kinston, Lorenzo and Mikki were relaxing in the tub.

"You gonna call Travis to see what he wanted?" Lorenzo sat with his back against the wall and Mikki between his legs.

"Nah. He'll be fine. Besides, since you're spending the night with me I don't have any time for him."

"And I bet we'll be up all night fucking and having fun," Lorenzo grinned.

"That's what I want and why I suggested we get this room. I couldn't take the risk at my place because either Travis or Kahneko could pop up," she told him.

"Hey! I got a question. You ever had anal sex before?"

Mikki laid her head back on his shoulder and closed her eyes. "Nope."

"Did you like it?"

"Can we please change the subject. Better yet, can you massage my boobs for me?"

Lorenzo chuckled. "One of us needs to go out and get some more condoms." He slid his palms over her wet luscious breasts.

"I got the food this morning so it's your turn to run an errand. Mmm… keep rubbing my nipple just like that."

Lorenzo kissed her under her ear with both hands tenderly stroking her heavy tits. "I made up my mind."

"Ummm, I'm listening baby."

"I'll hustle the pills for you."

"That's a good move."

"Maybe. But I think we might have a small problem."

Mikki opened her eyes. "About what?"

"Well, now that I've gotten a shot of your million dollar pussy, I'm not too easy with sharing you with Travis."

Mikki giggled as she wiggled her butt against his penis. "Stingy aren't we? Let me put it like this, baby. Stick with me and you'll be out from under Travis and PBH."

"What about Kahneko?"

Mikki shrugged. "She'll be okay."

Lorenzo had no regrets on his choice to rock with Mikki. When they got out of the tub she willingly took his disk back inside her wet mouth. She did it slow, taking all of him down her throat while caressing his ass. She was flicking her tongue over his balls when his cell phone rung.

"Who's calling?" she looked up at him with her hands stroking his spit coated dick up and down.

Lorenzo frowned. "Derrick."

Mikki paused for a split second. "Answer it."

"Nah. He ain't—"

"Please." She licked his tip. "I always wanted to do a guy while he's on the phone show me you can handle what I'm doing while you're talking."

Lorenzo's ego wouldn't allow him to back down from the challenge. As the phone chimed on the sink she licked his entire dick then circled her lips back around his tip. Lorenzo felt a tingle run up and down his legs as Mikki nibbled on his throbbing flesh. Showing off his self-control he answered the call as Mikki slurped between his legs like a porn star.

"Hey, what's up?" Derrick asked behind the wheel of La'Ashia's Benz. "Look, man, I know we ain't seeing eye to eye on some things and overall it ain't nothing too personal."

"I can deal with that," Lorenzo replied.

"Um, you gotta work today?"

"Nah. I'm off today."

Derrick switched lanes to pass a brown sedan. "Yo, we got a problem. I'm speaking on the issue about Goldsboro last month."

"That ain't good."

"Yeah... but it ain't nothing to break camp over."

"All right, so what is it?"

"I can't say how right this minute. But I was able to get a copy of the 911 call from that night."

"What are you talking about?"

"Somebody called 911 on us."

"Who?"

"Don't know yet. I haven't listened to the recording yet but I know for a fact somebody called. Anyway, I'm on my way to the crib to download the file off my iPad to listen to it. After that, I'm heading your way so you and Travis can listen to it."

"Uh, you talk to Travis yet?"

"Nah. He's at some bitch crib so you know the deal on that. You in Greenville right?"

"Yeah. I mean no... I—"

"Make up your mind," Derrick laughed as his suspicion went up a notch. "So where are you?"

"At the crib."

Derrick nodded. "Listen and this some real shit. I know Travis is fam, but I think he's sour."

"What!"

"I think he was the one that called 911. As for why I can't explain. We need to listen to the call, both of us. If it's him, we'll step to him about it and deal with it. Gimme about an hour and a half and I'll be there. You straight with that?"

"Shit don't make no sense, man."

"I know. But until we listen to the call, Travis is on the sidelines. But yo, I'ma hit you back when I reach Greenville. And if Travis gets there before I do, don't say nothing about this."

"What is going on with you?" Mikki hurried out of the bathroom behind Lorenzo.

"I'll explain it later. I have to bounce right quick!" Lorenzo jerked his shirt over his head then reached for his pants. *Damn! How the fuck did that nigga get a copy of my 911 call?*

"You're scaring me. Please tell me what's going on." She stood nude. "Did Derrick know you were with me?"

"No, it's something else."

"Just tell me! I thought we had an understanding, Lorenzo."

"I have to go, baby." Lorenzo's mind had to choose. Fight or flight were his two options.

Chapter Twenty Five

Goldsboro, North Carolina 7:55 p. m.

"Yo, La'Ashia!" Derrick shouted when he walked through the front door. "I'm back, and why don't I smell any food cooking?" He dropped his keys on the table in the living room then headed back to his bedroom. *Ass probably taking another bath again.* "Don't trip on me 'cause I gotta head back out to—" His words came to a halt when he entered his bedroom. He blinked three times, thinking his eyes were fooling him. La'Ashia was naked and tied to one of the kitchen chairs at the foot of the bed. A pair of her panties were stuffed in her mouth and covered with a strip of tape. She jerked at the ripped sheets that were tied around her wrists and ankles.

Derrick took three steps then froze. *What the fuck!* He thought instead of pulling out his Glock 45.

"Get down on the floor muthafucka! On your knees and put them hands on your head... nice and slow," a muffled voice ordered. "And don't even think of going for your gun!"

Derrick stared across the bedroom at a short figure dressed in black. She eased out of the closet gripping a black Taurus .380. Derrick placed his hands on his head and fell down to his knees. *Ain't this a bitch! Getting robbed by a bitch!*

"Don't think of anything stupid," the girl warned as she maintained a safe distance from Derrick. From her position, she covered La'Ashia and Derrick with the .380.

"Just tell me what you want." *I'ma give this bitch whatever she wants.*

"What's the combination?"

Derrick blinked, then glanced over toward the dresser. It was pulled from the wall. *Oh shit! My safe!* "Huh?"

"Pretty boy, don't make me repeat myself! Last time... what's the combination? Play games and I'ma make your bitch suffer!"

"Chill, chill, chill! The numbers are 9-14-18."

"Now stay on your knees and move over to the safe!" she gestured with the assault rifle. "And keep your hands on your head!"

Derrick moved sluggishly across the floor as La'Ashia started to cry. The voice wasn't known to Derrick and with the ski mask covering her face she remained nameless.

"All right, here's the deal. I want you to open the safe with your right hand only. Leave the safe shut then take those cuffs off the dresser and put 'em on."

Derrick nodded with a knot twisting tighter in his stomach. "Why?"

"Ain't come here to talk! Do what I said or I'll slump you and your bitch. Now hurry up and open the damn safe nigga!"

Derrick clenched his jaws in defeat. Of all his hard work and risks taken with his hustling behind bars, it all came to this. With a shaky right hand, he turned the dial on the safe. 9-14-18.

"Okay, it's open." He reached for the iron cuffs.

"Click 'em down tight!"

Derrick cuffed himself then watched the girl out the corner of his eyes. She stood beside La'Ashia with the silencer two inches from her left ear.

"How much is in the safe?" she shouted at Derrick.

Derrick lowered his chin. "$85,000."

"That's all? And I thought y'all PBH dudes were balling. Nah… there's more here so come up off it."

"I… I got a stash spot in the kitchen. Take it all, please. Just—"

"How much and where is it?"

"Behind the dishwasher is seventy more bands, yo. That's all there is I swear."

"For your sake, you better hope it is."

***

Lorenzo pulled into Travis' apartment complex at 8:10 p.m. with the headlights off on his SUV. Driving slow around the lot he searched for Travis' XTS and Derrick's Charger. After two passes, he backed into an open space then jumped

100

out into the night. He couldn't meet up with Derrick because he had made the call to 911. As he rushed up the steps to Travis' apartment, his choice was set to rob Travis blind.

***

"So you forgive me or what?" Travis asked Michelle as they sat alone inside his XTS.

"All I want you to do is to be a part of your son's life," Michelle replied from the passenger seat. "It's my only concern. It was never about the money."

"Uh, you got any plans for tonight?"

"I have a man." She crushed his hopes with a touch of enjoyment. "Do you want to meet Rikeith?"

"Sure. Just name the place and the time."

An uneasy moment of silence filled the sedan. Michelle crossed her arms then she glanced to her right. She could see Shayla talking to someone on her phone in the rental.

"I… should get going. I know Shayla is tired of waiting on me."

"When will I hear from you again?"

Michelle shrugged. Her thoughts jumped back to the one wild night she shared with him. She kept it real and shouldered some of the faults to some degree on how she got pregnant by him. When the condom popped, she didn't make an effort to encourage him to pull out. *I was so stupid back then!* Clearing her throat she looked him in the face.

"Why didn't you stop?"

"Stop what?" Travis asked with a puzzled expression.

"When we had sex. Why didn't you stop when the condom popped?"

Travis wasn't sure if Michelle was serious or not. "What kind of question is that? I mean, it's not like either of us wanted the condom to break."

"But you kept going," she insisted. "You knew the risk, but it didn't stop you."

"Shit… it ain't like you were any help when it popped."

"Do you regret it now?"

Travis sighed. If he could change the past he would, but today it wouldn't matter. The child was his, and he would have to face the responsibilities that came with being a father. Deep down, his main concern would remain on PBH. For a second, the idea of getting to know Michelle crossed his mind. Baby mother or not, she was still a born stunna in his view.

"Regret ain't gonna get nothing solved between us." Travis reached for her hand. "Let's make peace and take care of our son."

Michelle knew he was full of shit. His stance had turned too quick for her to believe him. "It won't happen overnight."

She pulled her hand away, then reached for the door. "I really have to get going."

"Wait."

Michelle had one foot out the door when she looked over her shoulder. "What is it?"

"Uh, you still taking child support out on me?"

Michelle snapped. "I knew your ass was fronting! All you care about is having to pay child support or not! And you—"

"Nah it ain't—"

"Don't interrupt me when I'm talking! Not once did you ask to see a picture of your son, so it shows you don't care. I gave you more than enough chances to make things right, but I see I'm wasting my time. And FYI, I love my son, but I regret I ever fucked with your sorry ass! I'll see you in court!"

***

"What the fuck?" Travis muttered when he later pulled up to Derrick's crib in Kinston. The night lost its cover from a dozen flashing lights atop the Kinston police cars and one ambulance sitting in front of Derrick's spot. Travis assumed the PBH run had come to an end and his intentions were to keep his foot on the gas. His intentions changed when La'Ashia stepped out the front door with two female paramedics at her side. Seeing Travis' XTS, she screamed his name, and then she broke out running to the street. Her sudden actions gained the attention of the police, the worst thing for Travis. He had no choice but to stop. *Fuck! Stupid ass bitch!*

La'Ashia yanked Travis out of his car with tears streaming down her face. Under a light pole, she clung to him with her face buried in his chest. A white male plainclothes detective stood on the curb with a suspicious gaze on Travis.

"What happened here?" Travis asked the detective as La'Ashia continued to sob uncontrollably.

"And who might you be?" the detective asked with his arms crossed.

Travis had nowhere to run even if he wanted to. "Travis Dixon. My cousin lives here. Now can somebody tell me what's going on?"

The detective relaxed his posture, then broke the bad news about the home invasion and Derrick being shot. Travis lost his cool. The detective tried to ensure Travis the gunshot wound to Derrick's leg was minor but Travis didn't take his word.

"Sir, we need to know what was inside those two safes. Can you give me some insight?"

Travis told the detective to do his fucking job before he sped off to the hospital with La'Ashia. Travis ran three stop signs in his rush to reach Derrick. Along the way, he made a handsfree call to contact Derrick's mom. The second his call was connected he learned she had already been reached by the police and headed to the hospital. Ending the call, he glanced at La'Ashia balled up in the seat crying.

"Talk to me," he encouraged. "I know you didn't tell the police shit, but I need you to calm down and tell me what happened. Who did this?"

La'Ashia wiped her face. "Some bitch!"

"A female? Who?" Travis shot a suspicious glare at her.

"I don't know!" La'Ashia sobbed. "I was in the bedroom cleaning up... and I heard a noise. Something like a window being broken. Shit happened so fast. I went to see what was up, and some bitch in all black was standing by the back door with a gun in my face."

"A bitch, huh?"

La'Ashia nodded. "I couldn't do a damn thang. I was so fucking scared... thought I was gonna die."

"Is Derrick okay? Where was he shot?"

"In the leg. He tried to rush the girl in the kitchen and she shot him." La'Ashia answered with tears rolling down her face.

Travis slowed for a red light two blocks from the hospital. With anger in his tone, he asked La'Ashia if all the money was taken.

"Fuck that money!" she cried. "You better be happy Derrick isn't dead! It's behind this PBH shit y'all got going on. Now look at the trouble it's causing. I kept telling Derrick to leave that mess alone."

"Fuck you mean, fuck that money! Your ass wasn't yelling that bullshit when Derrick was spending cake on you. My cuzzo got that bread from the mud and now you trying to dismiss it!"

"Fuck you ok!" La'Ashia screamed. All of this is your fault. I hate you!"

Later that night, Derrick made it out of surgery at 10:40 p. m. Travis had to holler at his cousin alone and that moment came when Derrick's mom and sister went down to the cafeteria.

"What's up, cuzzo?" Travis stepped inside the private room with a worried look on his face. Derrick was laid back with his left leg hung up in a cast.

Derrick managed a smile as Travis closed the door. "I got caught slipping."

"How's your leg?" Travis stood beside the bed with his hands on the rail.

"I'll walk again if that's what you're wondering. Doctor said it was just a flesh wound. Hurt like hell though when the bitch popped my ass."

"Man, what the fuck happened?"

Derrick sighed then told Travis how the lick went down. "Bitch took every penny I had stashed."

"The money can be replaced, so don't sweat it. We can—"

"I got hit for one hundred and fifty-six bands, cuzzo!" Derrick winced from a sharp pain that shot up his leg. "Somebody know about this shit, and I want to find out ASAP."

"You ain't gonna do nothing until you're back on your feet, so let me handle this."

Derrick balled up his fist. "What about Lorenzo? Did he call you today?"

"I haven't spoken to him, why?"

"I did what I said I was gonna do."

"And what he say?"

"Nothing much. Said he was at your crib, but I think he was lying through his teeth." Derrick shifted slightly on the bed. "Leg throbbing like hell," he complained.

"You sure he said he was at my crib? He's supposed to be at work."

Derrick nodded. "Something ain't right with that dude. Word on everything, if he has something to do with this I'ma—"

"Chill, fam." Travis glanced at the door. "Don't speak like that up in here. I'll get up with Lorenzo when I get home."

"We can't let this bullshit ride!"

"We won't," Travis said as he thought about what he knew concerning La'Ashia. If the info was true, it placed La'Ashia on the hit list.

"Why you looking at me like that?" Derrick asked.

"Just thinking about something. I don't see why you're putting so much trust back in La'Ashia. Did you tell her about the two stash spots?"

Derrick frowned. "Bruh, I know damn well you ain't tryna put this lick on my girl!"

"Can you gimme some proof she wasn't a part of it? Ain't no need to get hot with me, so face it, fam!"

"La'Ashia had my fucking combination okay! If she was gonna run me it would not be like this so think about that."

It made sense to Travis. "My bad, yo."

"Damn right it is! Where she at anyway?"

"Downstairs filling out the paperwork to be able to visit you. Since you got shot only family are allowed up here." Travis figured it was best not to bring up the topic of Derrick dipping off to Atlanta with La'Ashia.

"She's a trooper, fam," Derrick co-signed. "But yo, I gotta come clean about something dealing with your new baby momma, Michelle. Just promise me you won't get upset."

Chapter Twenty-Six

Selma, North Carolina 10:22 p. m.

Later in the night, Lorenzo sat inside his SUV with the engine running and the lights off. Looking up the street, his attention locked on the Range Rover Sport parked behind Shayla's gray Altima. He assumed she had another man up in the crib. He punched the steering wheel then glanced over at the two suitcases piled up on the passenger seat. All hell would fall on his shoulders as soon as Travis realized all his money was gone.

"Fuck this shit." Lorenzo's mood was ready for whatever. He needed to talk to Shayla and the moment was now. After locking up his Explorer, he jogged up to Shayla's front door while keeping an eye out for Travis' XTS.

***

Shayla and Michelle were in the living room talking about today's crazy events when a knock sounded at the front door. Shayla jumped up from the sofa and took notice of the time on the flatscreen TV. She wasn't expecting any company tonight at 10:30 p. m.

"Who is it?" she asked.

"It's me."

"Me who?"

"C'mon, Shayla, I need to talk to you."

109

Shayla quickly unlocked the door when she realized it was Lorenzo. The two hadn't laid eyes on each other since the day he left last month on the twelfth. His sudden appearance pushed Shayla off guard. "What are you doing here?" she asked, her heart racing.

"I came to talk," he said, "but I see you have company."

Shayla crossed her arms. "Why didn't you call?"

"Figured you wouldn't answer. So what's up? You want me to come back after old buddy leave or what?"

"That's your main problem. Why do you have to assume the wrong things all the time?" She frowned.

Lorenzo looked over his shoulder. "Who driving the Range Rover then?"

"Who was that bitch that answered your phone last month? You ain't gonna pop up at my door like it's all good between us. You were the one that left me and a day later you had another bitch answering your fucking phone!"

"I didn't come here to argue ok. I know I fucked up—"

"What do you want?" Shayla stood fixed in the doorway.

"I want to talk to you, please."

For the sake of their past, she stepped aside so Lorenzo could enter. His curiosity on Shayla's company was quenched when Shayla introduced him to Michelle. After the brief exchange of words between Shayla and Michelle, Lorenzo followed Shayla back to the bedroom.

"Never thought I'd feel like a visitor in my own home," Lorenzo mumbled as Shayla flopped down on the foot of the bed. When she didn't answer, he took a chance to sit next to her. "Where Alonso?"

"With my mom."

"I saw him last week while you were at work," Lorenzo offered. "I left some money with your mom, also."

"I know."

Lorenzo glanced around the bedroom looking for any signs of another man's presence. Living without Shayla were the moments he didn't wish to continue. The sex with Mikki and Kahneko held no weight when it came to being with Shayla. All of their problems were rooted in money but now his issues were worse. Seeing no signs of another man filled Lorenzo with relief.

"How did we end up like this?" Lorenzo asked.

"By you running out on me!" Shayla replied as she fixed he hair into a ponytail.

"And I was wrong for that. I... just couldn't take the thought of you being with another man."

Shayla sighed and shook her head. "I would never in my life cheat on you. Can you say the same in return?"

Lorenzo averted his eyes to the floor.

"That's what I thought!" Shayla vented. "And how long were you fucking this other girl?"

"I… it was only after I left you. I know it doesn't change much, and I'm sorry for what I did."

"Why did you leave me like that? All over a damn bikini that you tossed in my face and assumed some bullshit behind it. Well, you know what? Part of it is my fault because I was in the wrong, too."

"So you're going to tell me about the bikini?"

Shayla was tired of hiding. She was stripping to pay her bills and to support her son, and in her view, she was still justified. "I was stripping. That bikini you found was an outfit I had worn the night before and that's the truth. There was never another man in my life, and I'm still hurt that you could even think that I would do you like that."

Lorenzo wanted to blank out on Shayla for going behind his back. "Why?"

"We needed the money."

"Baby, you knew how I felt about you doing that—"

"How you feel isn't what keeps our bills paid. All right, I shouldn't have snuck behind your back, but I did it, so deal with it."

"I can't believe this," Lorenzo complained. "All you had to do was talk with me."

"I tried that, remember?"

"Are you still stripping?"

Shayla nodded yes. "I definitely have to since I'm the only one under this roof."

"How long were you gonna keep it behind my back?"

Shayla shrugged. "It doesn't matter now."

"Why not?"

"Because you're the one that has moved on."

Lorenzo reached for Shayla's hand. "It ain't gotta be like this, baby."

"No." She pulled her hand free. "You've been gone for over a month and plus you've been fucking with another bitch. I can't let you back into my life just because you realize your assumptions were twisted."

"I understand how you feel and I can't argue with you on what I did. All I want to do is make things right for you and my son."

"And how do you supposed to do that? If anything, things are worse now."

"You never had any type of faith in me." Lorenzo reached inside his front pocket and pulled out a wad of cash. "You don't have to strip no more."

Shayla looked at the money. "We can't make it off loans from Travis."

"Baby... I need to trust you on something." Lorenzo stood. "Promise me you will never give this money back."

"Give it back?" She frowned. "What's going on and where did you get it?"

Lorenzo sat back down then came clean with his dealings with Travis and PBH. He told Shayla everything, including what happened in Goldsboro. At first, she doubted his story, but her views changed when he mentioned the $375,600 sitting in his SUV.

"I've seen Derrick kill two… three guys in one night! Once Travis finds his money is missing I know he'll suspect me," Lorenzo told Shayla at the end of his story.

"Are you fucking crazy!" Shayla stared at Lorenzo. "Why didn't you go to the police or something?"

Lorenzo signed. "I can't do that." He shook his head.

"How could you get mixed up in all this?"

"Money. I did it to help us out but I got in over my head. Listen, I'ma get missing for a minute until it dies down. I need you to put the money up and if Travis ask about me you never saw me."

"I don't know about—"

"Just do it!" Lorenzo shouted. "We need the money more than he does so fuck that nigga!"

"That ain't true. Michelle has a baby by Travis."

Lorenzo paced the floor. "That ain't my concern."

"She's my friend. Travis might not be shit but robbing him will affect Michelle in the long run. She's about to take child support out on Travis."

"It doesn't matter!"

"Why are you bring your troubles to me! I didn't tell you to do none of this dumb shit and now you want to drag me into it!"

"I can't give the money back."

Shayla held the money up. "I don't want this."

"Are you crazy? You're stripping for it, but now you wanna act like a nun."

"I said I don't want your money!"

"What about our son? At least let me put some up in a trust fund for him. It's for his future, how can you argue with that?"

Shayla thought of her son and the words Lorenzo had spoken. Securing her son's future would ease a heavy strain off her shoulders.

"Please take the money," Lorenzo pleaded. "Just in case, I don't make it out of this bullshit. Let me be at peace that my son will never lack for nothing.

***

"Put Derrick on the phone!" Travis said as he stood in front of his empty closet. Every penny was gone.

"Yeah what's up?"

"We got a big fucking problem."

"I'm listening."

"Who's in the room with you?"

"My mom and La'Ashia. Holla at me, what's wrong?"

"I got him, fam. All my bread is gone!"

"Where is Lorenzo?"

"Dude ain't here and my door wasn't kicked in so it had to be him. He's the only one that has a key."

"Shit!"

"I need a favor." Travis walked across the room and picked up his keys off the bed. "Ask La'Ashia if she can help me draw Lorenzo out. Ain't about to play games with this son of a bitch, so I'ma show 'im how to turn it up."

"What's your plan?"

"I'm going to Selma. He'll have a choice to make, gimme my shit back or his bitch ass can get it!"

"What if he's already over there?"

Travis looked at his P2279 on the dresser. "He just better come up off my shit. That's all I'll say over this phone."

"Man, dude is a major liability over our head. All I need to mention is Goldsboro."

"I'll handle it. Just tell La'Ashia I'ma call her soon, and she needs to step out of the room to speak freely."

"I gotcha. And, fam, please be careful. Lorenzo knows we're on to his sour ass."

***

La'Ashia yawned as she made her way past the rows of parked cars outside the hospital. When she neared a silver Volkswagon Passat with tinted windows she hurried around to the passenger side and slid inside.

"We did it!" Kahneko said when La'Ashia closed the door. "Hope your man is doing okay."

"Fuck him!" La'Ashia frowned. "You could've murdered his ass for all I care."

Kahneko looked at her friend to see if she was serious. "I didn't mean to pop him. But he tried to rush me while I was bagging the money up. I see you're looking a tad upset."

"Please don't get it twisted. Derrick don't mean shit to me."

"Okay. We just made a lick for a hundred and fifty-six grand and you don't look happy."

"I got some bad news." La'Ashia sounded upset.

Kahneko had too much to worry about. Had she slipped up and left some prints behind? Did someone see her leaving the crime scene? She had covered every inch of her skin and played her role perfectly. Before she worried herself to death, La'Ashia told her about Travis being robbed. It threw a knot into their plans because they were scheming to rob Travis as well.

"You're kidding me?" Kahneko said as La'Ashia glanced out the window.

"Nope. And from what Travis told me, he thinks Lorenzo has it."

"So we go and rob Lorenzo and get missing like we planned. I bet he is hiding somewhere, and he still trusts me. We don't need Travis to do this. If Lorenzo has the money, we can handle this tonight."

"Do you think he'll pick up?"

Kahneko grinned. "Only one way to find out."

"All right, do it. See if you can get him to meet you somewhere. And as late as it is, he'll think it's strictly a late night booty call."

***

When midnight rolled around, Derrick wanted to sling his smartphone against the wall. For the last hour, he couldn't reach Travis or La'Ashia. "Fuck!" he said through his teeth. Just as he started to press the call button for the nurse, a knock rapped at the door. Before he could invite his guest in, Mikki stepped inside.

"Hey." Derrick laid the call button down, expecting to see Travis with Mikki. When she closed the door he stared at her. "Surprised to see you here. Um... Travis with you?"

Mikki slid a chair up to Derrick's bed then sat down. "How's your leg feeling?"

"Numb," Derrick replied with a confused look.

"You're lucky that AR didn't take your leg off."

Derrick frowned. "How do you know I was hit with an AR?"

"I have my sources."

He looked toward the door. "Travis with you?"

Mikki didn't answer.

"You... how did you get up in here anyway? This is a private room and I know you're not on my visitor's list."

"What's important to you?"

"I think it's time for you to leave." Derrick picked the call button back up.

"I wouldn't do that just yet. Besides, I'm positive you'd like to know who robbed you for all your money."

Derrick waited for a few seconds. "I guess your sources told you that, huh?"

"Where's Travis?"

Derrick shrugged. "Ain't my job to keep up with him. Go ask your sources."

"You're no different than the rest." Mikki smiled. "Now I see why La'Ashia made you such an easy target. Do you even know who she really is?"

Chapter Twenty-Seven

Selma, North Carolina July 28th Sunday

Shayla had her bedroom door locked with $100,000 dump on the bed she counted twice since Lorenzo had left nearly thirty minutes ago. Her plan was to put up $75,000 for her son and use the rest to get on her feet. With Michelle still under her roof, she had to keep the money a secret. After spreading the money out evenly she hid all but $800 in her closet. Once she was done she went back into the living room with hopes that Michelle was ready to call it a night. To her surprise, Michelle was curled up on the sofa talking on her cell phone.

"I accept your apology, but what you are asking isn't a good idea. And it's too late." Michelle rolled her eyes, then press the mute button. "Travis wants to know if he can come over?"

Shayla had to think fast. *I can't act too suspicious toward Travis. Damn, I hope like hell Michelle didn't tell Travis about Lorenzo's visit.* "Let me talk to him for a second."

Michelle gladly handed Shayla the cell phone.

"Do you know what time it is, Travis?" Shayla tried to sound friendly, even though her heart was jumping.

"Yeah, I know it's late, but I really need to talk to Michelle about my son."

"Where are you now?"

"Still in Kinston with Derrick," Travis lied.

Shayla looked at the time on her cell phone; 12:45 a. m. glowed on the screen. She assumed Travis hadn't discovered his money was missing. "Look, you can come over, but it's only to talk. Y'all ain't about to be doing no freaky shit up in my house and I mean it."

"Nah, I wouldn't disrespect you like that. But seriously, I really need to straighten my face with Michelle before she goes back to Miami."

"Whatever. Just remember what I said and I'll tell Michelle the same. I plan to be in the bed by the time you get here."

"Don't make me hang up in your face, so stop playing!"

"Just fucking with you. He should be at work anyway."

"Or at your crib laid up with another bitch." Shayla handed the phone back to Michelle, then stomped off to her bedroom.

***

Lorenzo figured times wouldn't be so hard on him with $275,600. Having left Selma behind, he was back on the road thinking of his next move. Mikki had called him six times in the past two hours. His third I told him not to trust her. *Hell, she fucking me behind Travis' back, so no telling how shifty her ass is. Pussy good though.* Lorenzo knew she had the room in Kinston, but the risk ran too high of being spotted by Derrick. If he could change it all, Lorenzo would wish to be back with Shayla and struggle instead of running off with Travis' bread. He had his SUV cruising down I-95 South when Kahneko called. On the third ring, he answered it using the hands-free Bluetooth system.

"Yeah?" Lorenzo answered.

"Hey, honey!" Kahneko's sexy voice jumped from the speakers. "You're a hard man to get up with. What has been up since we last saw each other?"

"Ah, about two weeks."

"Is everything good?"

"Yeah, it's all good. It's just my work schedule keeps me tied up, that's all."

"That's such a shame because I've been thinking about you lately."

"Oh yeah? Too bad you're two hours away in Havelock."

"Says who?"

"You're home, ain'tcha?"

"Wrong. FYI, I just happened to be at the Hilton in Raleigh. My BFF is coming to visit me tomorrow from Miami. I think our plane will be at the airport around ten a. m. Why don't you swing by and hang out with me?"

Lorenzo eased off the gas as the next exit off the interstate drew closer. Going to see Kahneko placed a roof over Lorenzo's head and gave him time to plan his next move. "I thought Mikki was your BFF?" Lorenzo switched lanes to make the exit.

"Can't a girl have more than one BFF?" Kahneko asked. "So do I need to wait up for you or not?"

"I'll be there.'

"Good. Stop by the store and get some condoms."

Lorenzo laughed. "For what? We haven't been using any."

"I've missed one of my birth control pills, that's why. I know I got that priceless kitty and I do love that raw dick. But right now I'm not ready to be a mom."

"I can understand that."

"Good. And trust me, baby, my pussy will be so wet and tight I'll still have you moaning out my name when you get up in it."

Lorenzo grinned. "Show me better than you can tell me."

"Won't be a problem, handsome, just bring me what I need and I'm in room eighteen."

***

"This plan is stupid!" La'Ashia argue with Kahneko. "We should just rob his ass as soon as he steps foot in here!"

"What if the money isn't on him?" Kahneko countered.

La'Ashia lifted a black .22 pistol. "Put this on his nuts and he'll talk."

Kahneko rolled her eyes. "Fire that thing up in here and we're both going down. Just let me handle it. Shit, look at how things popped off with Derrick's slow ass. Pussy is a man's downfall so it won't change with this lame."

La'Ashia place the .22 on the bed and grabbed the duffel bag stuff with money from the floor. "Just don't drag this out because I'm tired as hell. I've been up all damn day."

"It'll be over soon, and you'll forget all about the crap we've been through to get this money." Kahneko got up off the bed and grabbed a smartphone.

"I hope you don't intend on fucking Lorenzo when he gets here."

Kahneko walked across the plush carpet barefoot toward the bathroom. "And why wouldn't I? Don't forget about that dick you've been getting from Derrick."

"That was different you know it! I have to play wifey for him for this shit to work."

Kahneko sighed as she came to a stop and turn around. "Thirty minutes is all I need to get off. Let me do me and I promise will leave Richard."

La'Ashia folded her arms. "We're pressing our luck as it is."

"Just thirty minutes."

La'Ashia sighed. "It's still stupid. But I see I have no choice but to let you do it."

"Why don't you hide in the closet and watch us?" Kahneko grinned.

La'Ashia rolled her eyes. "I'll pass on that. But how about I call down to room service and have them send a bottle up here."

"Good idea. And see if they have any Moet." Kahneko smiled then twirled on her toes then slipped inside the bathroom.

"Stupid bitch," La'Ashia gripped under her breath. She had risked too much to let things fall apart just because Kahneko wanted some dick. With a building ill mood, she made the call down to room service as Kahneko turned on the shower.

***

Kahneko stepped out of the steamy shower at ten minutes pass one in the morning. The eight-minute shower had her feeling perky and ready for sex. As she reached for the towel, she saw an unread text message on her smartphone that was lying on the sink. By voice command, she opened the text and read it while she dried off.

The Moet is on ice. I'll B down in the lobby and U got 30 min! The $$ is in the closet and please don't fuck up.

Kahneko deleted La'Ashia's text only a mere second before Lorenzo called. She allowed it to ring five times before she picked up.

"Thought you weren't coming," she wrapped the towel around her head.

"Just wanna make sure you're still up. I should be there in about fifteen minutes. So it's still all good?"

"Yep. And did you stop for some condoms?"

"Yeah. I got'em."

"How many?"

"Enough to last us."

"I hope so." She stepped out of the bathroom. "Sorta have a feeling that we'll be up doing it for a while. I just hope you can hang with me and my sex drive."

"I'll show you better than I can tell you when I walk through that door."

"I hear you talking, baby," Kahneko replied. "When you do get here we can just let our actions do what it do. I got us some Moet to sip on, too; and this bed, we can get real nasty on it."

Kahneko milked Lorenzo with her raw talk of sex. In her view, she saw no type of wrong by mixing business with pleasure. Robbing niggas was a business, but fucking them was a pleasure she couldn't pass up. Before Lorenzo arrived she checked the closet to make sure the duffel bag was in the closet. After that task was done she slipped into a pair of green cotton panties and a white tank top that exposed her flat stomach. She checked the room twice over to make sure nothing was out of place that would tip Lorenzo off to the lick. Once she was satisfied she picked up a compact .380 off the night table, clicked the safety off then slid it under the pillow.

***

Lorenzo knew Kahneko would question the suitcase he carried but he figured he could tell her anything but the truth. He had leaned toward leaving the money in his SUV while he was up in the room but the risk was too costly. Reaching room 18, he knocked on the door with hopes that he could somehow come out on top with the issue dealing with Travis and PBH.

Kahneko greeted Lorenzo at the door with a glass of Remy in her hand. She smiled at him then motioned for him to come inside. "What's with the suitcase?" she asked after he sat it on the floor by the bed.

"Uh, just a few of my clothes and stuff that my ex was gonna throw out."

Kahneko glanced at the suitcase for a second then closed the door. "Want something to drink?"

"Yeah, might as well."

***

At the same time back in Selma, Travis was a mile away from pulling up to Shayla's crib when he received a call from Derrick.

"What the hell are you doing up so late?" Travis slowed his XTS to cross a pair of railroad tracks.

"Fam, we got bigger things to handle!"

Travis sighed. "What now?"

"Where are you?"

"On my way to see Michelle at Shayla's house."

"Is La'Ashia with you?"

"Hell no. She ain't never call me back. Had me waiting at—"

"You need to come back to the hospital."

Travis crossed the tracks then drove toward the stop sign ahead. "Man, I'm like two minutes from knocking on Shayla's door. Lemme check things out first and then I'll swing by on my way back."

"Fuck that! Just listen to me before you do something stupid. Lorenzo had nothing to do with this, okay!"

"Oh yeah? So I guess it's just a damn coincidence that that bitch ass nigga and my bread is missing, huh?"

"Just hear me out, man... damn! Okay... I'm not really sure if Lorenzo took your shit or not but I do know this one fact."

"And what's that?"

There was a brief pause from Derrick. "You were right about that dirty ass bitch, La'Ashia."

Travis slowed to a stop at the stop sign. His grip tightened on the steering wheel. "What did she do?"

"I gotta speak to you face to face, cuzzo." Derrick's voice came flat from the speaker.

"Ain't got no time for any games!" Travis barked. "Between the two of us we are minus half a fucking mil and a few stacks! If I have to beat Shayla's ass or whatever... I'ma get my gotdamn money back. Fucking tired of these games!"

"Cuzzo, don't be stupid. You moving real reckless right now. But real talk, you gotta trust me on this, fam. Don't go to Shayla's."

"Just tell me what's up with La'Ashia." *Probably what I already know!*

"I can't do it over the phone."

"Somebody in the room with you?" Travis asked as a pair of headlights grew in the rearview mirror.

"Uh."

"Man, ain't got time for these games, so I'ma—"

"You need to calm down and listen to what Derrick is trying to tell you," came a new, but familiar voice through the speakers.

Travis stared at the CUE screen as if he could see the owner of the voice. There was too much confusion going on for one night. "Mikki? Is that you?"

"Yes. And if you ever want to stand the chance of seeing a penny of your money again, you'll turn around. The choice is yours and you only have an hour to get here!"

Travis had no choice but to make a U-turn. Whatever plans he had of seeing Michelle and Shayla would have to wait.

Chapter Twenty-three

"Bitch, I swear to God you won't get away with this grimy ass stunt you pulled on me!" Were the first words that Lorenzo was consciously aware of when he woke up fully dressed on the floor in room 18. Rubbing his face he sat up and stared at the bathroom door as Kahneko continued her heated conversation behind it.

"Damn, I'm tired as hell," Lorenzo murmured as he used the arm of the sofa to rise to his feet. Looking across the room he saw the sun peeking through the drapes. *Why was I on the floor?* He reached down for his smartphone but it wasn't in his pocket. Frowning, he turned to look around on the floor. By his feet, he saw the box of condoms. Unopened. Something started to tug at him as being fucked up. Why hadn't he used any of the condoms and why was he still dressed? Behind him, he could still hear Kahneko going off in her one-sided phone call. He assumed she had his smartphone and some answers to what was going on. *I hope I didn't fall asleep on Kahneko.* He yawned then fought the urge to lower his eyelids again. When their eyes met he saw nothing but wildness. Kahneko was fully dressed in a pair of black, skinny jeans and a simple white tee. Her eyes were narrowed, her lips tight. When

Lorenzo stood she took a step back and raised her .380 at his chest.

"Whoa whoa whoa," Lorenzo tried to calm Kahneko down. "What—"

"Shut the fuck up and don't try nothing funny!" Kahneko said. "How much money was in that suitcase?"

Lorenzo couldn't take his eyes off the gun in Kahneko's steady grip. "Wh-wh-what money?" he stuttered.

"Don't play games with me right now because I'm two seconds from popping your fucking wig! Now how much gotdamn money was in that suitcase?"

"$275,600."

"And you stole it from Travis, huh?"

Lorenzo nodded. "Are... you holding me here until he gets here?"

"You're so fucking stupid." Kahneko shook her head. "Do you even know what is going on? From the looks of it, you don't."

"Yo... if you want the money it's—"

"Gone!" Kahneko blurted then gestured with the .380 for Lorenzo to sit down. "We both got licked by the oldest trick in the damn book. The money is gone, honey. And I'm about to do the same in just a minute. But before I bounce, I'll need you to kindly come up off the $100,000. Don't look surprised,

132

nigga! I know how much Derrick had in his stash and the same for Travis. Is it in your ride."

"I… don't have it." Lorenzo feared for his life but in no form would he place any danger on Shayla's doorstep.

"You wanna have a reason to live?" Kahneko kept the .380 leveled off at Lorenzo's chest. "Lie to me again and I'll make your bitch ass suffer! You just robbed Travis last night so I know you haven't blown $100,000 so… wait!" She smiled. "I know where the money is. Last night you told me you went to see your ex. She has the money?"

"No… but I can get it for—"

"So you lied to me! You should have told me the truth on round one, honey."

"What is all this about? I'll get the money to you… just leave my girl out of this," he pleaded.

"Wanna hear something funny? How about that slick ass hoe, La'Ashia drugged our drinks last night. We're both broke now and I didn't even get the chance to get some dick last night. Karma is a bad bitch ain't she?"

"So what do we do now?"

"*We* ain't going to do shit. What you're going to do is get your little bitch on the phone so she can come up off that money. I fucked up by trusting La'Ashia so I'm not in any mood to play any games. Here, make the call and don't try anything foolish." Kahneko tossed her phone on the bed.

133

"Make it easy on yourself. All I want is the money and I'll let you and your girl live to see tomorrow. Now make the fucking call."

***

"Why didn't you tell me about Kahneko from the start?" Travis questioned Mikki down in the parking lot in front of the hospital.

"Because I wasn't too sure what she and La'Ashia were planning to do. Like I told you last night... I din't know she was talking about robbing you and Derrick when I overheard her talking on the phone," Mikki explained as Travis stared at her.

"Why didn't you answer my calls yesterday?" he asked squinting from the rising sun over Mikki's shoulder. "I called you damn near three times."

"I was at the spa," she lied. "Besides, I was planning to come see you anyway."

Travis couldn't believe the scoop on Kahneko and La'Ashia being stick-up queens. Mikki had told him and Derrick all that she knew about Kahneko and La'Ashia but it was no place near the truth.

"Where would they be now?"

134

Mikki shrugged. "There's no telling. Kahneko hasn't answered any of my calls since Friday night. I'm sure they're on the move with the amount of money they have."

"Fuck!" Travis turned and walked a few steps from Mikki. "Why are you helping me?"

"Why wouldn't I?" she replied to his back. "You've been real with me since day one and I don't get down on no slick shit. You gotta trust me. If I could have stopped this I would have done so."

Travis turned back around with the sun in his face. "You got any ideas?"

"Do you want to get your money back?"

"That's a stupid question. You know I want it back."

"You might have to get your hands dirty."

"If you know something you need to tell me."

"It's not what I know. It's an idea that I have."

"What is it?"

"Do you trust Lorenzo?"

Travis frowned. "Fuck no!"

"I'm glad you feel that way, because he tried to holler at me one night. And before you trip, I didn't tell you because I didn't want to mess up any deals you had going with him and PBH."

"That's a bullshit excuse! If the nigga was grimy like that you should have told me from the jump. All of this could have been avoided!"

"I didn't know how to handle it, Travis."

"Fuck all that. What else do you need to tell me that I should have known? First, it was La'Ashia and Kahneko and now it's some shit with Lorenzo. Kill the games and just tell me how I can get my gotdamn bread back!"

Mikki glanced at the stylish gold watch on her wrist. It was seven minutes pass 9 a.m. "Go home and get yourself together and I'll call you around noon."

"Nah." He shook his head. "Ain't going nowhere until you tell me what the fuck is going on."

"You don't have a choice, okay. If you want my help it has to be my way or you can forget about your money."

Travis balled up his fingers into a solid fist. "Word on everything... I better not find out that you have anything to do with this bullshit!"

***

Moments later, Mikki sat inside her Infiniti G37 with the engine running. As soon as Travis peeled out in his sedan she made a call.

"Yeah?" a male voice answered after the second ring.

"It's a go," Mikki said. "Do you have a location for me?"

"Yep. We have a signal at an apartment complex in Durham."

"What about the other?"

"Still at the hotel."

Mikki scratched her chin. "That's odd. I assumed them two would stick together."

"It's your call. Do we move or not?"

"Let me call you back. I think I need to check on something first."

"You're going to Durham, huh?"

"Yes, but it stays between the two of us. But call me ASAP if she moves an inch."

"Not a problem."

Mikki ended the call then pulled out of the parking lot. She had her own agenda to focus on while maintaining a lie that she hope was well hidden.

She reached the highway to make the nearly two hour trip to Durham. With her focus set on a single task, she was never on point and didn't notice Travis' XTS tailing her at a measured distance six cars back.

***

Back in Selma, Shayla was in an ill mood from an early morning call that pulled her from under the covers. She viewed the unknown number on the screen then answered the call. "Hello?"

"Baby it's me. I'm so glad you answered."

"Lorenzo?" Shayla sat up. "Who's phone are you calling me from and why so early?"

"I don't have time to explain right now. But you have to listen to me, Shay. I… need the money back—"

"Have you bumped your head! How are going to bust my hopes by—"

"Shayla, listen dammit! I need the money back and it's not an option, okay. Just get the gym bag I gave you out of the closet and drop it off at—"

"You didn't—"

"Just do it!" Lorenzo shouted. "Get the gym bag and drop it off at the U-Store Storage unit in Clayton. Drive all the way to the back and drop the gym bag off in front of the last storage unit and leave. Don't wait for me or nothing. You have to do it now, baby. This is serious."

Shayla's heart started to pound in her chest. "Will you be there?"

"Just handle this, Shayla. I'm sorry I got you involved in this but you have to do what I just told you and nothing more."

"This is scaring me." She slid off the bed. "At least tell me you're okay."

"I'm fine. Don't worry about me. As soon as you do this I'll see you after it's over, baby."

"Promise me."

"I promise, baby. I... should of never walked out on you and I'm sorry."

Shayla walked over to the closet and slid the door open. The gym bag that Lorenzo spoke of sat in the corner to her right. "I forgive you. Just keep your promise to me and bring your ass back home to your family when this is over."

***

Mikki's Infiniti crossed into Johnston County just as her smartphone rung.

"What's new?" she answered using the hands free Bluetooth system.

"Our friend is on the move from the hotel. Heading east on Highway 70."

"And the other."

"Still in Durham."

Mikki switched lanes and sped up to 89 mph. "Why isn't she going to Durham?"

"Beats me. All I can do is tell you what the screen is indicating."

"Okay, what's her exact location?"

"Uh… in about six more minutes at the speed… she'll be in Clayton."

"What's the description of her vehicle again?"

"A new, silver, Volkswagen Passat. It's a rental, too."

"I already know that."

"Where are you now?"

"Heading west on Highway 70. If I continue my course I should make a visual on her."

"That's a chance. So… how do we do this?"

"Everything stays the same for now. If I can make contact with Kahneko I'll do so and just play it so. She doesn't suspect me for a threat to her so let's keep that in mind, okay. I just need you to cover things on your end before we close the curtains on this."

"My end is solid. I just hope you know what the hell you're doing out there."

Mikki eyed the oncoming traffic on Highway 70 East. "I'm doing what needs to be done," she replied. "Now watch that screen and talk to me until I'm within a mile of her. If she turns off the highway I want to know."

***

Lorenzo sat behind the wheel of the Passat with Kahneko directly behind him. He had little hope that the seat could slow

140

down a bullet. Kahneko had warned him twice that she wouldn't hesitate to pop his ass for any stupid stunts.

"Will you let me go once you get the money?" he asked driving at the posted speed limit.

"Shut up and drive."

Lorenzo squeezed the steering wheel. *I can flip us right now and take my chance with an accident. And with my bad luck, I'll fucking kill myself.* "How much did you take from Derrick?"

"Nigga, does it look like I'm pressed for any conversation? FYI, I'm not, so shut the fuck up!"

***

La'Ashia couldn't live in peace with Kahneko out for her ass. Reason number one, Kahneko knew too much and she would be driven to hunt La'Ashia down. La'Ashia was giddy when she found Lorenzo's suitcase filled with money. She now had a total of $431,600 packed in the trunk of the white Kia Optima that was five cars behind Kahneko's Passat. The Optima belonged to La'Ashia's cousin and it was unknown by Kahneko. La'Ashia's plan was simple. If she could catch Kahneko with her guard down she would use the .380 that sat on her lap. She had driven to Durham, switched cars then sped back to Raleigh to wait for Kahneko to leave. She figured something was up when she saw Lorenzo getting in the car

141

with Kahneko. It didn't change her plan. If Lorenzo was in the way, she would end his life just the same.

Chapter Twenty-Nine

"Drive around the entire storage unit one time," Kahneko ordered Lorenzo as he slowed for a speed bump at the entrance. Kahneko scanned the three rows of storage units as Lorenzo drove to the back. "You better hope your bitch did what you told her to do."

Lorenzo drove past the second row of storage units, then slowed for another speed bump. He hoped Shayla had dropped the bag off and left. When he neared the third row of storage units, he felt the gun pressed against his right ear.

"Do anything stupid. I swear I'll blow your mind!" Kahneko warned. "Bingo!" she said a few seconds later. "Is this your gym bag up ahead?"

Lorenzo kept his hands glued to the wheel. "Yeah." *Thank you, Shayla! Thank you!*

"Okay, stop the car."

Lorenzo eased down on the brakes a few yards from the gym bag to his right. He saw no sign of Shayla nor anyone else. They sat in silence for a few seconds.

"Here's the deal," Kahneko ordered, "we'll get out together and slow. Keep you hands on your head until you reach the bag. Once I see the money, I want you to bring it back to the car. After that, I want you to take off everything but your boxers, then walk over to the fence and sit the fuck down."

All was quiet under the partly cloudy sky as Lorenzo and Kahneko stepped out of the Passat. He wanted to try to overpower Kahneko, but he reasoned his chances were slim once she had the loaded gun.

"Do you want me to count it?" he asked, three feet from the gym bag.

"Just do what I told you to do!" she said in an icy tone. "If anything is missing you'll be the one full of regret and you can—"

Lorenzo ducked and fell to the ground when a loud gunshot went off. In total disbelief, he rolled over and found Kahneko face down with blood leaking from the back of her head. "Oh shit!" He stood just as La'Ashia walked up beside the Passat. He stared her down with fear of ending up like Kahneko.

"Don't even think about reaching for that gun," La'Ashia warned then glanced at the gym bag. "Is that what I think it is?"

Lorenzo couldn't take his eyes off the blood creeping toward his shoes. One second Kahneko was alive and the next she was laid out on the pavement. Without being told, he raised his hands high. "It's... the rest... Travis's money."

La'Ashia nodded. "Good." She adjusted her aim up toward his face.

"Please don't kill me." Lorenzo took a step back.

"How much is it?" she nodded at the gym bag."

"Uh… a hundred thousand."

"Pick it up and take it to my car. I'm parked near the entrance. Hurry up."

Lorenzo turned to grab the bag with La'Ashia standing a few feet away to his right. Whatever move he planned to make he had to do it without any hesitation.

With the gym bag strapped over his left shoulder, he made the short walk to the front of the storage unit with La'Ashia a few steps behind him.

"You need to walk faster! I don't plan on being here when the police show up."

Lorenzo quickened his steps as he neared the second row of storage units. Up ahead he saw the Kia Optima parked near the first row.

"Why did you take Travis's money?" La'Ashia asked. "I thought you were tight with him."

Lorenzo shrugged. "Just going through some hard times I guess."

"Put the bag in the back seat." La'Ashia stepped around the car with the gun pointed at Lorenzo. "The door isn't locked."

Lorenzo placed the gym bag inside the car then closed the door.

"Now back up against the fence and keep your hands where I can see them."

Lorenzo backed up slowly until his back hit the fence. He stayed in one spot with both hands in the air. The moment La'Ashia sped out of the entrance Lorenzo ran back to where Kahneko was laid out on the ground and searched quickly for her smartphone.

***

Mikki was a block away from the storage unit when her smartphone buzzed on her lap.

"Talk to me," she answered after the first time.

"Where are you?"

"Clayton and I—"

"Turn around."

"Why? Has Kahneko left?"

"Worse. Just overheard a 911 call about someone being shot."

"Who made the call?" Mikki asked as the light turned red up ahead.

"A male and he didn't leave his name."

"Shit!" Mikki slowed to a stop behind a black Ford Mustang. "So you're saying Kahneko's signal is still at the storage unit."

"I'm looking dead at a strong signal and it's not moving. Just take my advice and shut down before you make a mistake. I can only cover you so much on my end."

146

"I'm too close to back away from this, Scott. I can pull this off, please give me a little more time with this."

"I don't think that would be wise. Match the risk with the amount of the funds you can recover. What are we talking about... half a million and—"

"I'm aware of the risk—"

"I can't do it and that is my stance."

Mikki took a deep breath. "Scott, don't take this away from me okay. Look at all I've done for you. Have I lied to you before? No. If I say I can pull it off I can do it," she pressed. "Listen... how about I up your cut to 30%?"

There was a brief pause before Scott spoke. "You got 24 hours and that's it and not a second more."

"This will be over today and I promise you."

"I don't want a promise," Scott replied. "Just make sure you get my 30% and keep your hands clean."

Mikki ended the call just as the sounds of approaching police siren reached her ears.

***

Lorenzo had jogged a block and a half away from the storage unit when the first of three police cars arrived. He slowed to a brisk walk but kept his eyes ahead. No one paid him any attention as he moved about his own business along the sidewalk. Cars sped up and down the two-laned road while

Lorenzo thought of his next move. With each step, he reflected on his fucked up situation and the path that he chose to get where he stood. Facing reality, he laid the guilt on himself for assuming the wrong things about Shayla. Next, he was filled with regret for allowing Travis to entice him with the easy hustle in PBH. All he wanted now was to get to Shayla and his son. Lorenzo sped up when he saw a gas station up ahead across the street. Just as he attempted to dash across the street, a horn blew behind him. Turning with the sun blazing in his face he came to a stop as Mikki drove by. He stood in place as she made a quick U-turn and drove up to the curb.

***

"Why are you following me?" Lorenzo got right to the point as Mikki pulled away from the curb.

"What makes you think that?" Mikki asked. "I was just—"

"Cut the bullshit!" Lorenzo shouted. "Ain't no way you just happen to be in Clayton when all of this shit is going down. So what's up... you in on this bullshit with La'Ashia, too?"

"If I was you'd look real stupid for getting in the car with me. Besides, you're the one that needs to explain why you're on foot. Where's your ride?"

"Ain't gotta explain nothing until I find out what is going on!"

148

"You sure about that?" She glanced at him. "You can talk to me or I'll drop you back off at the storage unit. I'm sure there will be a homicide detective on site that would love to question you about Kahneko's murder."

Lorenzo stared at Mikki. *Oh shit! How the fuck did she know about that?*

"I can help you if you help me," Mikki calmly stated. "I must reason that you didn't shoot Kahneko... so who did?"

"You... wouldn't believe me if I told you."

"Try me."

Lorenzo lowered his posture in the seat as Mikki neared the storage unit. "Keep going."

"Not until you give me a name." Mikki eased off the gas.

"La'Ashia!"

Mikki stiffened behind the wheel. "She was at the storage unit?"

Lorenzo nodded. "I'm assuming you know her."

"What was she driving? Can you remember what kind of car she's in?"

"Yeah... um... it's a white Kia Optima. Now can you—"

"Shit!" Mikki stomped on the gas and made a call in the process.

"Can you drop me off?"

Mikki ignored Lorenzo as she headed toward Highway 70. Driving with one hand on the wheel, she motioned Lorenzo to stay quiet as the call went through over the speakers.

"Yeah?"

"Scott, pull up La'Ashia's file and tell me what info we have on her cousin in Durham. And please hurry!"

"What do you need?"

"What type of car does her cousin own?"

"Gimme one second."

Mikki turned on the hazard lights and sped past a beaten pickup truck. Ten seconds later, Scott confirmed what Lorenzo had told Mikki moments ago.

"La'Ashia is driving her cousin's car," Mikki told Scott. "She has to be going back to Durham and I—"

"How do you know this?"

Mikki glanced at Lorenzo, and then back to the road ahead. "I saw her leaving the scene, but I just wanted to be sure."

"Where the money?"

"It has to be in Durham."

"That still doesn't change anything. Jacqueline. By this time tomorrow, this case will be closed. With or without the money, now are we clear on that?"

"Yes," Mikki replied through clenched teeth.

"Good. Now will you need any assistance with what you have going on now?"

"I'm fine and you already knew the answer to that."

"Doesn't hurt for me to do my job."

"Thanks… and please call me ASAP if that signal in Durham moves."

Lorenzo tried to piece everything together as Mikki headed toward Durham. When the silence grew too thick he shifted in the seat to face Mikki.

"Can you tell me what in the hell is going on?" Lorenzo waited.

Mikki didn't even bother to glance in his direction.

"Do you even care that Kahneko's dead?" Lorenzo asked.

"How much did you take out of Travis's closet?"

Lorenzo figured he could twist the facts until he knew the truth about all that was going. "I don't know what you're talking about."

Mikki rolled her eyes. "Don't fuck with me, Lorenzo. You're in over your head as it is and I doubt you want to make matters worse. Now how much money did you get?"

"Why does it matter? I don't have it."

"I can see that. So where is it?"

Lorenzo shrugged. "What… you plan on giving it back to your man?"

"I'm seriously not in the mood for any games! Now tell me how much you took and where is it?"

"Fuck you!"

Mikki chuckled. "Upset huh? FYI, I know what was took and when you took it. And $375,600 is a lot of money when it's tax-free. And when I add the $156,000 that was taken from Derrick... that's $531,600 and I want it."

"So you're down with La'Ashia on this?"

"Nope. Not even close."

"Yet you seem to know what's going on when I don't."

"Where's the money?"

"Why should I tell you?"

"Because you can trust me, honey." Her sarcasm reeked through her voice.

"Yeah right."

Mikki kept her attention on the road while searching for the Kia. "Do you want the truth?"

"What do you think? And why did that dude you were talking to call you Jacqueline?"

"What would you do for half a million?" Mikki asked. "Well, it's clear you'll rob your best friend and throw your career away. Funny how you did all that for $375,600. Do you regret it now? I'm still trying to understand why you did it when you would eventually earn your own."

"So you don't have all the answers."

"Oh but I will," she replied sure of herself. "I guess when I connect all the dots it will take me back to Goldsboro. I'm sure you'd like to keep your name out of that triple homicide investigation that's going on. Wouldn't look too good for you to be a suspect in Kahneko's murder now will it?"

At that point, Lorenzo knew Mikki had a rope around his neck that he could not loosen. Whatever he had to do to avoid going to prison, it would get done. With that in mind, he told her the truth starting with his trip to Travis's home. At the end, he added. "La'Ashia slipped something in our drinks, and when I woke up the money was gone." Lorenzo slid a hand down his face. "All I wanted was to help my family. All this PBH shit, I just got caught up."

Mikki had allowed Lorenzo to speak without any interruptions. She took the news of La'Ashia having all the money as the perfect scenario that would meet her objective. "Okay, I guess I can be sensitive since you told me the truth," she said. "Pop the glove compartment, then look inside my clutch bag."

Lorenzo did as she asked and swallowed his words from the object he held in his hand.

Chapter Twenty Five

"What the fuck is this?" Lorenzo asked as Mikki swerved into the left lane on Highway 70 West.

"It's a badge."

Lorenzo glance at Mikki then stared at the FBI badge and her picture. "This can't be real," he murmured shaking his head.

"It's authentic and I wouldn't bet on it not being real if I were in your shoes. Now before you hit me with a ton of questions I won't answer let's get one thing straight. All I care about and want is the money."

"And I told you I don't have it."

"That remains to be proven. But until I get it, you're stuck with me, got it."

Lorenzo tossed the FBI badge on the dashboard."So your real name is Jacqueline D. Loh?"

She nodded."But that's Special Agent LOH to you."

"So... you're working undercover because of PBH?"

"No questions, honey. Just know that when I get all the money I'll be a memory. On the other hand," she cracked a smile, "It'll be better if you can just forget about me. If you don't want any more trouble."

"How does this end?"

Mikki shrugged. "Depends on one or more factors."

"How do I fit in?"

"Up to your neck."

"Look I just want to be done with this okay. I didn't kill Kahneko if that's even her name. And I—"

"Save the sob story because you're not innocent, okay."

"It's not a sob story!"

"Just sit back and enjoy the ride and you better hope La'Ashia has the money. And please don't try anything stupid."

***

La'Ashia couldn't stop herself from joyously dumping the contents from the gym bag on the bed. The hundred thousand dollars produced goosebumps all over her arms. With her cousin in the living room and oblivious to her actions, she quickly counted the money then added it with the $431,600 she already had in the closet. Her next move was to leave the state and start over with $531,600 to her name. Killing Kahneko placed no weight on her conscience. She didn't wish to split the money in the first place. It had all been her idea from the jump to rob Derrick after he showed her his ass when she tried to be in a serious relationship with him. When she discovered his hustle with PBH, it was then she thought up a plan for Kahneko to hook up with Travis. Things were thrown in a twist when Mikki ended up meeting Travis at the club. Kahneko had waited too late to push up on Travis but managed to befriend Mikki that same night just to stay close to Travis. While the plot formed, La'Ashia and Kahneko played their parts perfectly. *Men are so dumb,* La'Ashia thought as she wrapped a rubber band around a stack of cash.

In thirty minutes she had the money repackaged inside a pink oversized gym bag. Everything was peachy. She didn't give a fuck about anyone but herself. Just as she zipped the gym bag closed, her smartphone chimed on the dresser behind her. When she glanced at the screen she was surprised to see Mikki face and number. *What the hell this bitch want?* La'Ashia wondered. She had never been to find out if Mikki and the fake friendship Kahneko was forced to deal with had become something more. She pressed the ignore icon, determined to be on the road within the hour.

***

Mikki kept her focus down the street on La'Ashia's Benz as her call went unanswered. *Okay, so this trick want to play games with me. All I have to do is stick back and wait until she steps up with the money.*

"Can I use your phone?" Lorenzo asked breaking Mikki's thinking.

She paid him no mind.

Lorenzo sighed. "I just need to call my girl and let her know I'm okay."

"Not going to happen," Mikki replied as she rode her eyes.

"How long are you—"

"Shut up I'm thinking," Mikki cut him off. Her mind was was running on ten as it stood with each wasted second. She needed that money. Every last penny. An idea popped in her head. *Alright, she won't answer my call, but she'll nine times out of ten read my text. Got to send something to get her attention.*

Lorenzo weighed his risk of jumping out of the car as Mikki busy herself with the smartphone. *Not got to see this bullshit to the end. Running won't help me none. I know Shayla is worried sick about me.* Lorenzo calmed himself to sit still. Looking up ahead, he to place his attention on La'Ashia's sporty CLA Benz. *If I make it out of this I swear I'll never do no wrong by Shayla.*

***

La'Ashia was inches from the bedroom door when she received an alert for the text message. Reluctantly she pulled her phone out the heavy gym bag and dropped it to the floor. The message on the screen instantly tied her stomach in a knot.

We need to be rational about this. I know what you did to Kahneko and I bet the police would enjoy talking to you. That can all be avoided because we can meet on a common ground. What do you say to a split of that $531,600? You have 60 seconds to hit me back. Or I will call 911 and we will see how fast they can reach you at your cousin's crib in Durham.

The fear of going down for Kahneko's murder shook all the fight out of La'Ashia. With a shaky finger, she touched the call icon to speak with Mikki. Unable to stand, she sat at the foot of the bed with her heart thumping in her throat.

"I was ten seconds from calling the police on your ass," Mikki taunted the instant the call was connected. "I assume you're speechless but all I need to hear is a yes or no. Do you have the mullah?"

La'Ashia glanced at her bag of future on the floor."Yeah, I have it."

"I figured you did. And the amount is what I put in my text right?"

"How did you—"

"Bitch, answer my goddamn question! Tell me the numbers," Mikki demanded.

La'Ashia had no idea how Mikki was up on her game. She had talked to no one about laying low at her cousin spot. For that reason, she was not in the position to bargain or doubt Mikki's threat of calling the police. She told Mikki the correct amount that she had in the bag.

"That's what I wanted to hear, "Mikki replied. "Now about our split. Is it cool with you? Of course it is because I know you don't want to go to prison for murder. So now we need to come up with a nice and clean exchange of what you have. Keeping in mind what you did to Kahneko, let's just say that I won't turn my back on you. Now tell me who is in the apartment with you?"

"Just my cousin. But she has nothing to do with this."

"Do you have all the money now?"

"Yeah."

""Listen to me, okay. Bring all of it outside and sit on the curb—"

"Wait! I thought you said half?"

"I changed my mind. Or you can keep it all and see how much a good lawyer will cost these days. I'm giving you something far greater than money. Your freedom should be the first thing on your mind at this point, don't you think? I wouldn't think on it too hard if I were you."

"How do I know you won't call the police after you have what you want?"

Mikki laugh. "News flash. Bitch, *I am* the police! How else have I been able to stay two steps ahead of you? You can't answer that, can you? Well, I'll put you up on the whole shebang. Last year you and your former partner in crime, Kahneko used your talents on a hustler up in Jersey City, remember that? Robbed him for eight bands and fucked up my entire case and more. See, I had my eyes set on all of his bread, not that chump change you and Kahneko took. You two dumb, penny-chasing tricks cost me seven fucking million! So now I'm freelancing, and I knew it wouldn't be long until you moved again. I've been on you since day one. You owe me, and I will gladly relieve you of that paper."

It all makes sense now. La'Ashia thought back to a late night call she had gotten from Kahneko about five weeks ago. Kahneko claims she had overheard Mikki on the phone through the bathroom door at Travis's apartment. She said it sounded like she was working on a scheme to rob Travis and Derrick. La'Ashia simply told Kahneko to chill since she couldn't speak on anything specific to lay caution to this game. La'Ashia was narrow-minded and focused on that PBH paper. Now it was too late to dwell on the shoulda, woulda, and coulda. She stood on her own now, forced to deal with Mikki and keeping her ass out of prison. If Mikki was being honest, La'Ashia figured she could find another sucker-for-love ass dude with bread down the line. Her only drive was money, and with her looks and talk game, a baller didn't stand a chance against La'Ashia . She told Mikki she was on her way out the door. *Fuck this money.* La'Ashia headed to the front door with the gym bag.

***

160

Mikki shifted her Infiniti out of neutral when she saw La'Ashia stepping out of her cousin's apartment. "I got my eyes on you," Mikki warned. "Just chop the bag on the curb then you go back inside."

Lorenzo could see the fear in La'Ashia's posture two blocks up the street. He cut a glance at Mikki, making sure her attention was focused up ahead. Something had to give, he wasn't ready to run another mile with Mikki or whoever the hell she was. When she ended the call he looked back up the street and saw a large, pink bag on the curve. Mikki checked the rearview mirrors then pulled from the curve.

***

"Something isn't right." Shayla had tried to call Lorenzo six times in the last 20 minutes.

"We should go to the police if you really feel he's in trouble," Michelle suggested as she slowed for a red light on Highway 70 in Clayton. "We've been riding around all morning and you still haven't told me what's going on. I'm sure you didn't have me drive up here to drop off a bag of clothes." Michelle hated to be nosey but it was clear that something serious was going on.

"I can't call the police. If I do I might make matters worse than they are right now."

"If your man is in trouble you need to be smart about it," Michelle replied.

Shayla wanted to snap the smartphone in half when her call went unanswered again. *How can I trust her?* She reasoned. She might have the nerve to flip on me if she learns Lorenzo robbed Travis. *I got to do something!* "Can you call Travis?"

Michelle rolled her eyes. "For what? FYI I stayed up real late for him and he was a no-show. Why would I waste my time calling him?"

"Just call and see if he'll answer." Shayla was worried that Travis was the reason for Lorenzo not answering his phone.

Michelle slid the figurative strand of hair away from her eyes. "Can you at least tell me what's going on? I thought we were friends."

Without a second thought about Lorenzo safety, Shayla had to go against her better judgment. With tears forming in her eyes, she came clean and told Michelle all that she knew of the Lorenzo's thievery.

***

Mikki had instructed Lorenzo to unzip the gym bag the second he jumped back inside the car. Satisfied with the contents, she sped from the curb.

"Okay, you got what you wanted. Why am I still being forced to roll with you?" Lorenzo asked with the heavy bag of money in his lap.

"Funny how this is ending isn't it?" A wicked smile formed on Mikki's lips. "You robbed Travis and then you got caught slipping by Kahneko and La'Ashia. Your luck isn't worth shit if you sit back and look at it. I would love to be a fly on the wall when you and Travis meet back up. I doubt he'll believe a word of what you'll tell him. And knowing how he thinks, he'll assume you had something to do with his cousin being shot and Rob."

"This shit is funny to you!" Lorenzo for the first time in his life had the urge to smack a female.

"Actually, it is. And there is not a goddamn thing you can do about!"

***

"Man what the fuck!" Derrick complained. "I've been calling your ass all morning and I—"

"Fam you won't believe what I've seen this morning," Travis butted in as he steered the XTS with one hand. "I've been following this bitch Mikki since we left the hospital."

"Word? What's the 411 behind that?"

"Long story. But listen at this. I been on this bitch all morning and guess who she picked up in Clayton?"

"Tell me."

"Lorenzo of all people. I swear I wanted to confront them both but something told me to fall back—"

163

"That nigga fucking Mikki?"

"Man who gives a fuck about that! All I want is my motherfucking paper. Listen, I tailed that bitch to a second spot and you ain't going to like this. But man, I saw your girl La'Ashia. That's some grimy ass shit. I don't know what the fuck is going on but I promised to find out ASAP!"

Chapter Thirty One

Greensboro, North Carolina

"Why we stopping here?" Lorenzo asked as Mikki pulled up at the Hampton Inn in Greensboro.

"Just a little stopover before I'm on my way," she told him. "All I need you to do is to get the room in your name. Do this and you'll be free to run back home to your girl."

"And if I don't?"

"Baby, you don't have no bargaining chips so stop wasting my time!"

Lorenzo chained his temper in check as Mikki slowed to a stop near the front lobby. She tossed a fresh hundred dollar bill on his lap and ordered him to hurry up.

***

Travis sat across the four-lane main street with a clear view of the Hampton Inn. He couldn't ignore the small twinge of jealousy behind his thoughts of Lorenzo and Mikki creeping behind his back. *And I gave this Bama a place to sleep when he had no place to sleep!* Travis grabbed the .45 from under his seat. *Muthafucka think I'ma let this shit ride! Ain't no fucking way.* Travis was intent on getting his face back. Glancing at his watch, he noted the time. 2:40 p. m. Just as he settled back in the front seat in his XTS, his smartphone buzzed. The call went to voicemail after he saw Michelle's number.

***

"It's all here," Lorenzo told Mikki after counting the pile of money on his side of the bed.

"I don't need to count behind you, do I?"

"Do whatever you want. I'm just ready to get the fuck up out of here!"

"You don't have to be so vile. I'm not the one that got you into this mess."

"Yeah, but it ain't like you're helping me to get out of it!"

"I could've left your ass in Clayton to deal with the police." she reminded him.

Lorenzo stood. "You got the money, so why am I still here?"

Mikki picked up her smartphone and slid the back cover off. "You can leave." She removed the SIM card. "Or you can spend one last moment with me in this bed."

"Hell no!"

"What will you do?" She looked at him. "You will have to deal with Travis and Derrick and all of the PBH shit you're tied to. Face it, your life is fucked up and walking out the door won't help you one bit."

166

"Why do you care?" He frowned. "Oh yeah, it's all about the money."

"You still don't get it? Yes, it's all about the money, but you can't ignore all the pleasure we shared together. FYI, fucking you was not part of my plan."

"And you expect me to fall for that bullshit? I don't even know who the fuck you are! Whatever issues I have to face, I'll do it on my own because I see now that motherfuckers are out for self."

"It's a little too late to gain some morals, don't you think? Seriously, how are you going to smooth this over with Travis? You took his stash and his girl." She smiled. "I won't be around to tell him my side of the story, so we both know how that will turn out."

Lorenzo clenched his jaw. The urge to pound Mikki with his fist grew hot inside him. "This is all a game to you, ain't it! You don't give a fuck about me, so don't try to convince me otherwise."

Mikki stood across the room until she was up in Lorenzo's face. "You're right. I don't give a fuck about you, and I guess it is all about the money."

"Okay, you got what you wanted, now what?"

"Your problems are bigger than the beef you'll have with Travis."

"What are you talking about?"

"PBH is going down and it's not because of me. And before you say you don't care, I think you will since your plug is a snitch."

"Who?"

"Mac," she replied. "In truth, Sergeant Parker is using him to do her dirty deeds. From what I was told, she has a recorded phone call between Mac and Travis that she's planning to turn over to us."

"How is the FBI involved?"

"PBH is selling drugs and other items to gang members and that's a federal charge. I bet Travis didn't point out that risk, did he? Anyway, the point is this, my fellow agent Scott is working on the PBH case, but my angle is the money. La'Ashia and Kahneko have no idea who I am and it will stay that way."

"Fuck Mac! I don't even work out—"

"It doesn't matter where you work. PBH will be exposed and that's a fact. But if you listen to what I can offer, I can keep your name out of it."

Lorenzo shook his head. "A little too late for that. And besides, why would I trust your ass? You think I'm stupid!"

"It's not important what I think about you, so I'll be blunt. I'm leaving the country tomorrow, but I can't do so with Scott on my ass."

"That's your problem. Not mine!"

Mikki sighed. "Just hear me out! Scott and I have the same views when it comes to reporting the amount of drug money we recover."

"Y'all were skimming off the top?" Lorenzo guessed.

Mikki smiled. "And the bottom. We were put under a small investigation, but nothing was proven and that was four years ago."

"And you're still doing it?"

"Something like that. But I'm on my own, and Scott knows what I'm doing and he wants a cut of it."

"I assume you ain't giving him shit?"

"Now you're thinking."

"Okay, so you won't pay him, which isn't a surprise. How can you—"

"We have to kill him."

"*We!* Hold up! No fucking way will I have a part in killing a federal agent!"

"You don't have much of a choice."

"The hell I don't!"

"And I thought you were 'bout this life."

"Hold the fuck up! You're the police so how the fuck can you question how I move? By law, I supposed to mark your ass and—"

"Do it then!" Mikki shouted and snatched her gun from her waist. "I'll give you my gun and you won't do shit with it. Yeah, mark a federal agent in a room that's listed under your name. How long do you think you can run? A week? Two, three or four? You were never built for this shit. PBH pussy. You know Travis can't make it a single day on the streets!"

They stared hard at each other for several seconds. Lorenzo stood face-to-face with reality while making Mikki wait for him to respond.

"Ain't a damn thing pussy about me!"

Mikki shoved the gun in his hand. "You feel that power?"

Lorenzo took a step back and admired the chrome piece that Mikki had just handed him.

"You don't have the balls to pull the trigger," she challenged him.

"Wanna bet?"

"Matter fact, I do," she replied. "I bet that the next few minutes I'll have you digging my back out. You want to kill something," she taunted, "Kill this fat, wet pussy I got in these jeans." Mikki unbuttoned her jeans without taking her eyes off Lorenzo she kicked her shoes off and then pushed the jeans down her curvaceous hips.

Lorenzo lowered the gun. "What the fuck is wrong with you?"

"Ain't nothing wrong with me." She stepped free of her clothes. "I want some dick and you're going to give it to me."

"This is crazy!" Lorenzo shook his head. "I'm leaving."

"No, you're not." She took her top off then turn around. "You can't walk away from this ass. So don't front." She looked at him over her shoulder while rubbing all over her ass. "I have a new deal for you."

Lorenzo tried to fight his lust for Mikki with each breath he took. She had slid her panties halfway down her ass. His dick was just as hard as the gun he held.

"Make me come one last time and I'll let you go. Don't tell me you can't do it—"

"Shut the fuck up!" Lorenzo stepped toward the bed and missed the grand smile that formed on her face. She was right. He couldn't turn down her offer of sex.

Mikki enjoyed every second of Lorenzo's heated lust. When she pulled his dick out of his boxers she dropped to her knees and swallowed it whole. His weakness was her strength.

***

Nearly three hours later, Lorenzo ogled at Mikki's bare ass as she went inside the bathroom. The sex had been nonstop and left both weak and satisfied. When the bathroom door closed behind Mikki, he turned his attention to the pile of money on the sofa. He sat up. Something had to be done.

Running would not solve this problem. That was one thing he had figured out as the day drew on. Fucking Mikki was a bitterness that made him feel like shit. Yeah, the sex was top-notch, but he was powerless to ignore the lust between them. He kicked the sheets off and reach for his boxers just as Mikki appeared in the bathroom doorway. She was stark naked with her hair flowing past her shoulders. He hated the sight of her but still held the urge to fuck her.

"Are you going to join me?" She prominently displayed her nutmeg-colored nipples.

"I need to talk to my girl," he forced his reply.

Mikki crossed her arms then nodded at the hotel phone on the night table. "Make it quick." She swayed her hips as she crossed the room and grab his soft dick. "I'll be quiet."

Lorenzo stood speechless as Mikki again dropped to her knees. She nuzzled her nose up against his balls before he reached for the phone. "I'm starting to enjoy doing this to you." She stroked his flesh up and down until it turned to iron against her chin. "We could make a good team."

Lorenzo ignored her comment as her soft hand sent chills up and down his spine. He wanted to shut her away and cut all ties with her. Just as she opened her mouth the phone rang on the night table.

"Who did you call?" she snapped as she stood.

"I didn't call nobody!"

Mikki stared at the hotel phone as it rang for the second time. "Don't lie to me!" she shouted.

"Just answer it 'cause ain't for me! You're the one that's running shit, remember?"

Mikki frowned. "Fuck this!" She snatched the phone up. "Hello?"

"What type of bullshit you on?"

Mikki gasped. "Travis?"

"Yeah, bitch, it's me!"

Mikki muted the call then jumped in Lorenzo's face. "Why did you call Travis and tell him we were here?"

"Get real! Why the fuck would I call him?"

"Well, how he get this room number?"

"You're asking the wrong one."

"Shit!" Mikki had to think. "I can't believe this," she muttered as Lorenzo had a good idea to get dressed.

"Don't be scared now," Lorenzo said. "You're the police, remember."

"Fuck you!"

Mikki took a deep breath and sat at the foot of the bed. She could handle this. "Who gave you this number?" she asked.

"Bitch, it don't matter! But I know one thing. You and that bitch ass nigga Lorenzo better come up off my bread!"

"I doubt that will happen."

"You fucking with the wrong one!"

"And I doubt that, too. In fact, you just might be fucking with the wrong one."

"Well, what, you think Lorenzo was going to save you? Both of y'all on some trifling ass shit but it's all good. He wasn't nothing but a sludge for the asshole anyway, but I'm two steps ahead of you and fuck ass Bamma in the room with you!"

"Is that what you think?"

"No, bitch! It's what I know, and I want my money!"

Mikki tried to show no fear over the phone, but deep down she was concerned about how Travis was on her. She had an idea. "See you got to take Lorenzo's word over mine? What did I you tell you?"

"Fuck him! When I see Lorenzo, shit is going to pop off! FYI, I've been on your slick ass since you left the hospital. I knew you were up to something! But you know what? I'ma still come out on top. I bet you, Lorenzo, and La'Ashia are all in on this bullshit."

"Okay, what's your next move? You know where we are, come on up and get what you want."

"Not, bitch, you going to come to me and on my terms."

"Oh really? And what makes you so sure of that?"

There was a silent pause between the two.

"There's an abandoned movie theater crosstown behind the mall. You and your loverboy need to be there within the hour with every goddamn Benjamin!"

"If we don't?"

"I'll just sit back and watch you deal with your colleague Agent Scott Walker. I bet he's feeling some type of way since you're running off with all the money."

The phone dropped from Mikki's hand. Travis was more than two steps ahead of her with his knowledge of Scott. She assumed she could handle Travis, but it would be a losing battle to go up against Scott and the bureau.

Chapter Thirty Two

Travis had complete confidence in his plan to get his money back from Mikki and Lorenzo. He stood hidden across the street from the Hampton Inn with a clear view of Mikki's car. He checked his watch, 5:18 p. m. Six minutes went by since he ended his call with Mikki. Just as he started to call her to see what was taking so long, he received a call from Derrick.

"Yeah, what up?"

"Ain't shit. Just laid up in this bed wondering why you're doing some backward ass shit!"

"Whoa, fam. I told you—"

"You ain't told me a motherfucking thing!" Derrick replied tightly.

"Man, I know you ain't tripping off of what I told you about La'Ashia?"

"Nah, it ain't that. I just had a special visit a few hours ago, and I want you to guess who the fuck it was."

"Ain't got time for this, fam! I'm trying to get our goddamn bread back, and you all up in my ass off some bullshit!"

"Nah, cuzzo, you're the one on some bullshit! What the fuck are you doing cutting deals with the fucking Feds?"

Silence. Travis swallowed the lump in his throat.

"Answer my question!" Derrick shouted. "I just had a little talk with that redneck FBI agent, Scott Walker!"

Travis shook his head. "Fuck!"

"Word up, tell me what that is—"

"Just hear me out though. Listen, remember when I told you about my funny feelings behind Mac fucking with Parker?"

"Yeah! But what the fuck does that have to do with the FBI coming to see me!"

"A lot. Now shut up and listen! Okay, back in early July, Agent Scott Walker popped up at my crib with the deal. Of course, I denied that shit. But yo, the dude is crooked, cuzzo."

"A deal?"

"Yeah. He put me up on game about Parker going to the FBI about PBH. He said he was in charge of the investigation, and to get to the point, he wanted in on our hustle instead of shutting us down."

"And what did you say?"

"What the fuck you think? He could've taken me down on the spot!"

"So you've been dealing under the table with the Feds behind my back!"

"I didn't have a choice."

"You could've told me! Now you got everything all fucked up. Your boy is looking for your ass, so I suggest you answer his next call."

"Fuck him."

"Nah, it ain't gonna be that easy, fam. How could you do something so stupid? Do you think that pig is going to keep us out of prison?"

"He can't turn us in, fam. He's in too deep with us, and this shit is going to end today."

"And how do you plan to do that? You don't even have your bread back from Mikki."

"She's another problem. The bitch is working undercover. Scott told me everything about her two days ago. It was his way of earning my trust. Plus he wanted me to be on point with the chance of her robbing me."

"And I see that didn't help at all," Derrick said. "Now even if you get our loot back, we still have the Feds on our ass. What about searching Parker and Mac?"

"You won't believe this, but Scott was talking about doing something to make Parker have an accident if you know what I meant."

"Now you're really talking stupid! Do you hear what the fuck you're saying? You expect me to go along with this bullshit? First, you cutting deals with the Feds and now I understand that y'all to plan to do something to Parker? Mikki must be smoking that good shit."

178

"Trav, man, I know I fucked up okay. Don't nobody in the Feds know about PBH but Scott and Mikki. As soon as he thought we were getting money he wanted in on the action."

"So him and Mikki are working together?"

"I don't think so. She's on her own mission. Scott told me it's some type of personal beef with La'Ashia and Kahneko. Them two bitches are stick up queens."

"And you figured it's the right time to tell me! After I was robbed! I could've gotten killed, cuzzo!" Derrick aggressively stated.

"Calm down—"

"Don't tell me to calm down! You knew about La'Ashia all along you didn't tell me shit. We supposed to be blood, yet you willing and dealing with the Feds like it's cool!"

Travis attempted to come up with the right words to justify his actions. "Listen, fam, I fucked up okay. Just let me handle it since I'm the one that stepped into this shit. I'm gonna get the bread back and I'ma handle all the loose ends so nothing can turn back on us."

"PBH is finished and you know it. What if Parker went to someone else besides the Feds? Have you thought about that?"

Travis sighed. "Worrying about shit we can't control ain't going to help us none."

"Where are you now?"

"In Greensboro. I followed Mikki and Lorenzo to the Hampton Inn."

"So you got a plan?"

"Yeah I do."

"I hope you know what you're doing."

***

Mikki moved quickly inside the room after she got dressed. With the gun firmly in her grip, she banged on the bathroom door. "You need to hurry up in there!"

A few seconds later the door open. "Why do I have to go with you?" Lorenzo asked as Mikki looked him up and down.

"What were you doing in there?"

"Using the bathroom!" Lorenzo was annoyed.

She stepped past him and sniffed inside the bathroom. "I don't smell anything."

Lorenzo smirked. "I guess my shit don't stink."

"You still think this is a game, don't you?"

"Look yo! I don't give a fuck what it is! You were the one that was in charge just minutes ago and now you—"

"Just shut up okay! Grab the money and let's get out of here."

"Fuck that. I ain't going nowhere. Firing that gun up in here will bring too much attention up here."

"Wanna bet?" Mikki raised the gun up to Lorenzo's chest. His whole character changed when he saw the silencer.

"That's what I thought. Now grab the money before I put your ass to rest."

***

At the same time in Raleigh, North Carolina, a phone rang on the third floor of the downtown FBI building. Special Agent April Bohman toyed with the idea of ignoring the call. "Agent Bowman," she answered after the sixth ring.

"Bowman, it's me, Wilson, down in—"

"I have caller ID agent Wilson." She rolled her light blue eyes.

"I have something hot, and I checked it out as best I could, so I hope you're still in your chair!"

"I'm listening."

"Five minutes ago one of our agents took a call on our main one 800 line. Some guy in Greensboro said he's being held against his will by a crooked FBI agent working undercover. Our agent that took the call said the guy sounded tense—"

"Get to the point, because I'm in the mind of this being a prank call."

"It's not. The caller gave up two names. He said the agent's name was Jacqueline D. Loh and she linked up with another agent that he only knows as Scott. I pulled up personnel files, and we have an agent by that name!"

"Go on."

"Well, I pulled up her profile, and I saw she's not what you would call a 'model agent.' She's been under internal investigation by the bureau for misuse of it evidence. In other words, she was suspended for filling her pockets with drug money before it was inventoried."

"Where and when did it happen?" Bowman asked wth deep interest.

"Four years ago up in New York. Word has it, we took down some heavy hitters in the Cartel and something like two mill came up missing."

"And this Agent Jacqueline D. Loh was on the case?"

"Correct. But here's the clincher. Guess who was also put under internal investigation with Loh? An agent by the name of Scott Walker. I don't believe it was a prank call and I'm pretty damn sure about it."

"What else do you have?"

"I did some research and found out the agent below is on an extended vacation."

"Which station is she assigned to?"

"Atlanta."

"What about Agent Walker?"

"Are you ready for this? He's assigned here. Been here for almost five months in the RICO division."

Bowman cleared her throat. "Where is he?"

"He's out in a bureau vehicle. If given the authorization I can—"

"Do it." Bowman decided. "Track his vehicle and keep me posted on his location. I don't want to alert this guy. I'm thinking he'll slip up and hopefully he will."

"What about the guy that called us? He also mentioned something about going to the abandoned theater near the mall. Just said we need to be there."

"In Greensboro?"

"Yeah."

Bowman reached for her badge. "Find Agent Scott Walker and leave the rest to me. I'll keep this as quiet as possible to find out what is really going on."

"You think he might not be working alone?"

"Something like that."

"What about the director?"

"I'll handle him. Have the agent that took the call keep his or her mouth shut. Can you take care of it without mine—"

***

"You have a phone?" Mikki jerked up in the seat. "Where is it?"

Lorenzo wanted to kick himself in the ass. *Damn, I fucked up!* Lorenzo passed her Kahneko's smartphone then waited for her to flip out.

"You were on the phone in the bathroom!" Mikki yelled. "Who did you call?"

"I didn't—"

"Keep your hands on the wheel!" Mikki pressed the silencer against his head. "Who did you call?" she asked again.

Lorenzo closed his eyes. Lying to Mikki was pointless. He had not been able to erase his call to the FBI. "I called the Feds."

"You stupid jerk!" She shoved the gun against his head. "I should blow your fucking brains out! Who did you talk to?"

"Some agent. I—"

"Just shut up!" Mikki checked the mirrors, they were still alone, but for how much longer she wasn't sure. "Drive off and take a right at the stop sign ahead!"

Lorenzo looked up the street just as a black Chevy Caprice pulled over to the curb about a block away.

"Wait!" Mikki's stomach twisted into a knot. "It can't be." She lowered the gun from Lorenzo's head. There was a bigger threat to face.

***

"I got it."

"Good. Now before I go, please text a picture of both agents to my phone and anything else you feel I should be aware of."

Special Agent Bowman's next move was a private call to the FBI office in Greensboro. As she explained the situation to the agent in charge, she asked for back up in the form of a few field agents. Agent Bowman no longer believed the call was a prank. Whatever was going down at the theater couldn't really be good. Ten minutes later, she lifted off the roof in the back of the helicopter. As the helicopter banked toward Greensboro, she had a pinpoint location of Agent Scott Walker's vehicle on her laptop. The GPS system worked, and it placed Agent Walker heading west on Highway 70, five miles from Greensboro. Whatever the future held for Agent Walker in Greensboro, Bowman wouldn't be there to see it.

"Hurry!" she said into the mouthpiece. "I need to be in Greensboro ASAP."

The pilot acknowledged her request with a nod.

***

Back in Greensboro, Mikki motioned Lorenzo to slow to a stop just a few yards from the abandoned movie theater. They parked across the street but kept the engine running.

"Now what?" Lorenzo asked.

Mikki glanced at the time on her smartphone. 5:50 p. m. "We wait," she replied. "He'll call me."

"Why don't we just toss the money out the window and bounce?"

We? Mikki frowned. "First off, that's not happening. And second, I have a plan. Travis is bluffing about calling Scott."

Lorenzo scanned the theater for any signs of Travis. "Well, I don't want no parts of it."

"Too late," Mikki said.

Lorenzo checked the rearview mirror. Nothing. No sign of Travis nor the Feds.

"Something isn't right," Lorenzo said seven minutes later. "Why no call from Travis?"

Mikki was having the same thought but she stayed quiet. She had to tie up the loose ends with Travis. She couldn't understand how he knew of her true identity. In all of her seven undercover cases, her cover had never been blown. *I'm missing something.* She thought as Lorenzo sat impatiently behind the wheel. Mikki pushed her thoughts back to her conversation with Scott. With greed between them, there wasn't any space for trust. Mikki relied on her training and the ability to remain calm. "Shit!"she muttered.

"What is it?" Lorenzo asked.

"I forgot my phone back at the room."

Lorenzo's mind was so focused on the moment that he made a mistake. "Here. Use mine—"

Chapter Thirty Three

Greensboro, North Carolina 6:18 p.m.

"That's close enough!" Mikki warned Agent Scott Walker when she stepped out of the car. "I got this under control. What are you doing here?"

"That gun isn't necessary." Walker slowed to a stop 15 yards away. "Aren't we on the same team, Agent Loh?"

"You're full of shit! What's up with you and Travis? Care to tell me why you blew my cover?"

"It's rather complicated, to say the least."

Mikki kept the gun lined up center mass on his chest.

"Put the gun down because you won't pull the trigger. All I want is my cut of the money. You owe me!"

"I don't owe you anything!" Mikki tightened her grip on the gun. "You crossed me by blowing my cover!"

"I was hoping it would not come down to this."

"Yeah. Well, that makes two of us, only I don't give a fuck."

Walker smiled. "Is that your friend Lorenzo in the car?"

"I'm not in the mood for this, okay!"

The smile faded from Walker's face. "Travis said you were running out on me. I had to see it with my own eyes."

"The money shouldn't be your concern, okay?"

"You're missing the big picture, Agent Loh. I can't let you take it. PBH is going to grow, and I'll be the one running the show. All I had to do was hang a RICO case over Travis's head and wahla, he broke down. We, you and I, can make millions on this prison hustle. That's the big picture."

"Why did you blow my cover!"

"The opportunity presented itself. When Sergeant Parker's statement about PBH came across my desk I intended to do my job."

"And why didn't you?"

"You were in the way."

"That's not true. I was after La'Ashia and Kahneko—"

"And you were still in the way gotdammit!"

"Why didn't you tell me?"

"The case was new. I didn't realize you were mixed up with PBH until you asked for that favor. When I put those trackers on La'Ashia and Kahneko's cars I almost bumped into Derrick. I know all of the members of PBH, including your friend in the car. I wasn't expecting him to rob Travis so—"

"Where is he?"

"Who?"

"Travis!"

"Cuffed and in my trunk. Care to talk to him?" Scott smiled.

Mikki shook her head. "No. What I care to do is leave."

"Not with my money you're not."

"This conversation is over. You can—" Mikki stiffened when she heard the sound of a low flying helicopter and sirens.

"Put the gun down before someone drives by and call the police."

"That's already been done," Mikki said.

"What do you mean?"

"Lorenzo called the FBI and—"

"You're bluffing. There is no way I'll fall for that lie."

"You can stand there and find out for yourself because I'm leaving."

"I doubt it. See, not only do I have a tracking system on your car, I also have a kill switch." Walker slowly reached inside his suit jacket and removed a small black device. "Looks familiar don't it?"

Mikki cursed under her breath. "We have to leave!"

"That's not going to happen."

"I could kill you right now!"

"And risk the chance of me disabling your vehicle."

The sirens grew louder.

"Don't make me do this!" Mikki screamed. "Just follow me and we can settle this some place else. We have to—"

"No! You can leave, but the money stays."

"You fucking idiot!" Mikki raged as she thought of her options. Could she fire a round that would kill Walker instantly? A head shot from 15 yards away with a silencer was a challenge. Falling back on her training she raised the gun and sighted in on Walker's head.

***

Agent Waker dove to his left just as Mikki fired. He rolled twice and returned fire with his Glock .40 caliber handgun. His unsilenced shots echoed off the face of the abandon movie theater. As he sought cover behind an oak tree he pressed the button on the kill switch. As the sirens and the helicopter drew closer he began to realize his mistake. Mikki had told the truth. He risked a peek around the oak. Lorenzo was forcefully attempting to get out of the disabled car. Knowing his own freedom was now in jeopardy his thoughts were no longer on the money. Just as he prepared to rush toward his car, the front windshield took a hit. A second later the left front headlight exploded. When it registered in his mind what Mikki was doing or trying to do, he screamed. "No!"

Mikki's fifth silenced shot blew out the front left tire on Walker's Caprice.

"Now we're both on foot, asshole!" Mikki shouted.

Walker kicked the trunk of the oak tree then looked up through the branches. The helicopter was only minutes away.

He thought of Derrick back at the hospital and Travis in the trunk of his car. Everything was falling apart. Accepting his defeat, for now, he retreated from the scene and on the wrong side of the law.

***

Thirty minutes later, Lorenzo and Travis were winded and hiding behind a dense foliage at a park. The two had placed as much distance from the movie theater as possible. They sat on a patch of dirt, catching their breath.

"I need to get to a phone to call Shayla to come pick us up," Lorenzo whispered as Travis fought to catch his breath.

"This don't change shit because—"

"I could've left your ass in the trunk!"

Travis stared at the cuffs on his wrist. "It's still fucked up how you went up in my stash!"

Lorenzo sighed. "Okay, I fucked up. But now it's bigger than that and you know it."

"Why did you come and get me?"

Lorenzo shrugged. "You're still my bro. I couldn't leave you stuffed in the trunk like that. The way I see it, we both got tricked by the same bitch."

"Still don't make it right what you did."

"Look who's talking. You're the one that was fucking with the Feds. I mean seriously man, you had the Feds involved with PBH! What part of the game is that?"

"Scott ain't no different from us! That motherfucker don't care about nothing but money, and I didn't have a choice. Everything was under control until you teamed up with Mikki, La'Ashia, and Kahneko."

"That ain't true."

Travis frowned. "And I'm supposed to go for that? I gave you a spot to rest your head and what kind of love do I get for it? You hit my stash and fuck my jump off. How was it done? You fucked La'Ashia, too?"

"Telling you a lie won't get me nowhere. I can face my fuck ups, can you?"

"You call this a fuck up! You schemed with that bitch La'Ashia to rob my cuzzo and got him shot—"

"Whoa. You got your facts twisted on that one. Ain't have a damn thing to do with what you're talking about. Kahneko said something about knowing what Derrick had in his stash but I never heard anything about him being shot and robbed."

"Well explain why I saw you this morning. I've been following you and Mikki since she picked you up in Clayton."

Lorenzo rolled over to his side then quickly gave Travis the entire story. He spoke the truth without a pause until he reached the part of La'Ashia killing Kahneko.

"La'Ashia shot Kahneko!" Travis exclaimed.

"Right in front of me. I thought it was was over for my ass too."

She should've shot your punk ass! "Okay, what happened next?"

Lorenzo continued to tell his side of the story. Travis' face was tight as he heard how his money had exchanged hands for the second time.

"Where is La'Ashia now?" Travis asked.

Lorenzo shrugged. "Shit, don't ask me," he replied. "But shouldn't you be more concerned about where Mikki is?"

"Bitch is on the run just like us."

"But with your money."

"Gotdamn right! *My* money and I won't let that chinky-eyed bitch get away with this!"

"She's a federal agent," Lorenzo reminded Travis. "And what's up with Scott?"

"Man! I wouldn't give a fuck if Mikki was the President's daughter! That bitch got my mutha fucking bread! When I catch her! Her ass is gonna get popped!" Travis frowned. "But real talk. Fucking with Scott is a different story. He ain't a man we want to go against." Travis added.

"I can believe that because Mikkie tried to talk me into merking him. That bitch is crazy."

"No, she ain't. She has all the money, and we're stuck behind this bush in the dirt."

Lorenzo nodded thoughtfully. "But at least we're free."

"Yeah, for now," Travis muttered. "And I got these funky ass cuffs on."

"Yo, she knows about Goldsboro, too."

Travis stared at Lorenzo. "That ain't good."

"You got any ideas how we can get out of this bullshit?" Lorenzo asked with a worried expression.

"You need to call your girl ASAP. You ain't still on her bad side, are you?"

"Nah, I'm good. But she'll come through for me if I can get to a phone."

Travis looked over his shoulder. "How about that store down the corner?"

Lorenzo rolled over on all fours. "You'll be okay here?"

"Bruh, I can't move around too much with these on." He raised his wrists and shook the cuffs. "All it will take is one motherfucker to see me and call the police. I'll sit my ass right here."

"Okay, I'ma go make the call." Lorenzo slowly moved to a crouch then brushed the dirt off his jeans. Just as he started to creep toward the road, Travis cleared his throat. Lorenzo turned.

"Yo, thanks for not leaving me back there," Travis murmured.

Lorenzo grinned. "It ain't nothing. You would've done the same for me?"

"We'll discuss all that later when I get these cuffs off. Now, go call your girl so we can get the fuck up out of here."

***

Nearly two hours later at 9:20 p. m., Shayla slowed her Altima near the basketball court in the rear of the park in Greensboro. "Do you see them?" Shayla asked Michelle.

"Blow the horn," Michelle suggested.

"Nah. I don't want to draw any attention."

Michelle shifted in the seat, then reached for her tote bag. "This crazy."

"What?" Shayla asked.

"All this mess. You said Lorenzo stole some money from Travis, and now they're on the run together. It just doesn't sound right."

"Trust me, I feel the same way."

"Well, I hope you know what you're getting mixed up in."

"I'm not worried too much about that. Lorenzo wouldn't—"

"Look!" Michelle pointed straight ahead. "That looks like Lorenzo!"

Shayla gripped the steering wheel to contain her relief. Lorenzo calmly made his way across a grassy field as if everything was normal. A few seconds, later he slid inside the Altima behind Shayla.

"Boy, what in the hell is going on?" Shayla turned in the seat.

"Some bullshit," he mumbled. "This is like the worst day ever!"

Michelle glanced over her shoulder. "Where is Travis?"

Lorenzo stared at Michelle then looked at Shayla. "How do she know Travis?"

"They have a baby together, remember," Shayla replied. "But he's with you, right?"

"Yeah." Lorenzo nodded. "Drive over near the picnic area and back up near the curb."

"Is something wrong with Travis?" Michelle asked.

Lorenzo was hesitant to talk to Michelle. He had truly forgotten about her link with Travis.

"Stop tripping," Shayla said over her shoulder.

Lorenzo didn't know what to say. Right now he had other issues to focus on.

"I'm not surprised… you don't know anything about me. Am I right?" Michelle asked Lorenzo as Shayla drove toward the picnic area.

"Uh, he told me about the DNA test and all that. But he never mentioned your name or told me anything about you."

Michelle rolled her eyes as she turned back around. "I'm not surprised."

"Does Travis know what you did?" Shayla was concerned. "I'm surprised to see y'all two together in light of what's going on. Can you trust Travis?"

Lorenzo sighed as he stared at his hands. "Yeah, he knows. But as far as me trusting him, I doubt I can do that."

"So, what's the next move?" Shayla asked as she turned into the park.

Lorenzo leaned back in the seat and spoke the truth. "I don't know."

***

Travis's heart pounded as he crept near the curb in a low squat. The moment he saw Shayla's car through a gap in the shrubs he wanted to bolt for it.

When he reached the edge of the shrubs, he stayed low and waited until Shayla made a U-turn. The park had been Travis's refuge for the past few hours, and he was ready to make it a memory. Just as Shayla slowed to a stop, he saw Lorenzo gesturing for him to make a break for the car. He jumped to his feet and hustled for the rear passenger side door with his shirt draped over the cuffs.

"Lord! What have you two done?" Shayla asked a second after Travis was inside the car. "Why do you have on—"

"Baby! Please get us outta here," Lorenzo pleaded. "We'll explain on the ride back home."

Travis was shocked to see Michelle in front of him. In truth, she was a stranger to him. Pushing Michelle from his thoughts, he shared an idea with Lorenzo.

"Ask Shayla to drive by the mall before we leave."

"The mall? What for?" Lorenzo asked.

"That's where I left my ride at when Scott caught me off guard. If it ain't there then I know he has it."

"Good idea. And I might have a scoop on Mikki. She took Kahneko's phone."Chapter Thirty Four

"Fuck!" Travis mumbled as Shayla turned from the mall's parking lot. "Motherfucker got my ride and my gun. I need to use a phone to call my car company headquarters." Travis glanced at Lorenzo with hopes he would get Shayla's phone.

"Baby, lemme use your phone right quick," Lorenzo asked Shayla.

She shook her head then glared at him in the rearview mirror. "You need to tell me what is going on!"

"Shayla, please! This shit is serious and I—"

"I'm serious, Lorenzo! Either you tell me what's up or your black ass will walk back to Selma. And the same goes for you too, Travis. What I want is the truth. Now!"

Lorenzo didn't have much of a choice and neither did Travis. Starting from the beginning they told Shayla and Michelle what was up. Having heard enough, Michelle dug inside her tote bag then handed Travis her smartphone. She didn't know what to take for the truth as Lorenzo went on with his side of the story. $531,600 was a steep amount of money, but not enough to kill for in Michelle's view.

"What did they say?" Lorenzo asked Travis when he ended his call.

"I told'em my nephew has my car and I needed to know his location."

"Did it work?"

Travis nodded with the smartphone on his lap. "Look."

Lorenzo slid over to view the screen. In a color detailed map, it showed Travis's XTS as a blue arrow heading east. "Where is he going?"

Travis shrugged. "I can't tell. But he's way ahead of us right now. About twenty minutes from Durham."

"You got a plan?"

"Fuck Scott. It's Mikki I'm after. What were you talking about her having Kahneko's phone?"

"Maybe we can track her with it? Call the phone company and report it missing or something." Lorenzo explained his idea.

Travis didn't think it would work. "You'll have to know the access code and all that other bullshit. Do you know it?"

"Nope," Lorenzo replied. "But I bet La'Ashia might have it. What's her number?"

***

"I told you not to answer any calls!" La'Ashia glared at her cousin from across the room in Durham.

"Relax. It's not the police, so stop tripping."

La'Ashia's expression stayed in a frown as her cousin tossed the smartphone on the bed. "I'll be in the kitchen."

La'Ashia sat at the foot of the bed. "Who is this?"

"Lorenzo."

"And what the fuck are you calling me for?" She frowned. "You and your little bitch got the—"

"It's not what you think, okay. I'm calling because we might can work together on something."

"Picture that!"

"I'm for real, yo! I don't even have the money. It was Mikki—"

"I don't give a fuck! I know what went down, so I'll just charge it to the game! We ain't got shit to talk about so don't call this number no more! And if I see you—"

"Did you know Mikki is working with the Feds? She told you the truth when she said she was the police. FBI, shit, it's the same. Do you wanna talk to me now? She fucked me over, too. She has the money and that's the only thing she cares about."

"What about her threat to call the police about Kahneko?"

"It was a bluff."

"And how did she know about what happened? Care to tell me."

"I told her."

"So now you're a fucking snitch! I knew I should of...." La'Ashia caught herself before she said too much over the line. "Listen, what's done is done. I did my dirt and I'ma move on so I suggest you do that same."

"Not if I have a chance to get my money back."

La'Ashia laughed. "You mean Travis' money. That's who you need to be worried about. Besides, I don't believe a word you're saying anyway. If it's true, good! That's what your ass get for being grimy."

"So you wouldn't act on a chance to catch Mikki slipping and get the money back?"

"You're wasting my time."

"All right, I got somebody else that wants to holler at you."

La'Ashia's patience grew thin but her curiosity was thicker. "Who?"

"What's up La'Ashia?"

La'Ashia's mouth dropped when she heard Travis's voice.

"Can't speak uh? I figured so. Yeah, you ran game real sweet like on my cuzzo but just like you, he'll charge it to the game. That's the code of the streets, right?"

"What do you want?" La'Ashia said once she found her composure again.

"I need your help. Everything Lorenzo said is the truth. The way I see it, we all have a common enemy, Mikki."

"Oh really. And you expect me to believe you'll forget about what I did to Derrick? Come on now Travis, I'm not even close to being stupid. I know how PBH get down. I don't need to bring up what happened in Goldsboro do I?"

"Nah. But that proves I have no reason to bullshit with you. But back to the reason of this call, can I help you?"

"Not until you tell me what is going on. How are you all bubbly with Lorenzo after what he did to you?"

"Long story that's not worth the time. All I want is my bread. He doesn't have it, so waste my time beefing with him, feel me?"

"Makes sense. But I'm still not convinced you two are being one hundred with me."

"I can understand that. But here's the deal. Some bullshit went down today and Mikki has Kahneko's phone. Well, we're hoping she still has it. Anyway, we need Kahneko's access info so we can call the phone company and report it stolen. We can use that GPS App to track the phone and—"

"I don't have it."

"Are you sure? I bet we—"

"I said I don't have it! I want that bitch too so trust me! If I could help you I would."

***

"She's telling a lie right through her fucking teeth!" Travis told Lorenzo after he ended the call with La'Ashia.

"I told you she would." Lorenzo kept his focus down the street. "If she can track Kahneko's phone, she'll be on the move real soon."

"I hope this shit works," Travis scoffed.

"Where is Scott?"

Travis pulled up the screen that was tracking his car. "Still on the move. Just left the city limits of Goldsboro. Still heading east."

"We need another car," Lorenzo said. "I don't wanna drag Shayla in this too deep. And La'Ashia has already proven how she's getting down."

"She didn't merc you," Travis said.

"Yeah and I bet she's regretting it too."

Travis signed. "How is this gonna end? Everything is all fucked up. Even La'Ashia know about what went down in Goldsboro."

203

Lorenzo looked at his watch. It was ten minutes pass 8:00 p. m. Up in the front, Shayla and Michelle stayed quiet. When Shayla covered her mouth to yawn, Lorenzo suggested that he should drive. It was a good idea to Shayla. Michelle loath the idea of the tiny space between herself and Travis. They were parked along the curb of a quiet two-lane street in Durham. Small two and three bedroom homes were lined up and down both sides of the street.

"So… you sell drugs?" Michelle forced herself to ask Travis.

"Something like that," Travis replied.

"And yet you work at a prison. How ironic."

"It works for me."

"Don't look like it." Michelle began to loosen up. "You're broke and stuck in a pair of cuffs."

"Who said I'm broke!"

"My bad."

Travis looked at Michelle and realized for the first time how beautiful she was. "Can I ask you a question?"

"What?"

"Um… can I see a picture of my son?"

In the front seat, Lorenzo was fighting with a choice. Continue to help Travis or fall back and go home with Shayla. His pride kept pushing and shoving him to ignore the later. *I can outsmart Mikki!*

"Baby, why are you doing this?" Shayla asked in a soft whisper. "Look at what you're doing. Look at all the mess you've been through in the past two days."

"I have to correct my wrong, baby."

Shayla shook her head. "Not like this you don't. What if that girl leads you on a false path?'

"She won't."

Shayla looked down the street at the driveway Lorenzo had pointed out to her. "I don't like the idea of you following her."

Before Lorenzo could respond, Travis tapped him on the shoulder. "Yeah?"

"We need another car," Travis said. "You said it yourself, right."

Lorenzo looked back at Travis over his shoulder. "I know but... yo! How did you get out of those cuffs?"

Travis pointed at Michelle. "She used a hair pin. But you, gimme a few minutes."

"For what?"

Travis reached for the door handle. "I'm going to steal us a ride."

***

La'Ashia paced back and forth with her mind split on her next course of action. She had lied to Lorenzo and Travis. The second she learned about Mikki having Kahneko's phone she knew Travis's idea would work. Only she would do it alone.

205

After a ten minute call with her phone service, she had the location of Kahneko's smartphone. Turning toward the bed she reached under the pillow and wrapped her hand around the .380.

***

Shayla pleaded with Lorenzo to stay inside the car as Travis blew the horn behind them.

"I'll be okay, baby. Just trust me, okay. I have—"

"It's not about trust! This is so stupid, can't you see? You're about to get in a stolen car with Travis and follow that girl to god knows where. What if it's a trap? And how can you even think about trusting Travis? Put yourself in his shoes."

Lorenzo was torn between listening to Shayla or following his pride. "I know what I'm doing, baby."

"You're wrong." Shayla wiped her tears away. "It's still the same. You're running behind Travis instead of standing on your own two feet. It's Travis's problem, not yours."

Shayla meant good, but her words twisted Lorenzo's pride. "Don't go there with me on that! I know I've fucked up and said the wrong things to you but I'll always be me. I have to do this. I can't rest with this bullshit over my head." He stepped one foot out the door.

"So you're leaving me again?"

"Baby, I—"

206

"Go! Just go and do whatever it is that's more important than me!"

Lorenzo reached for Shayla's hand just as Travis blew the horn again. Glancing down the street he saw La'Ashia's Benz backing out of the driveway. "This will be over soon, baby. If I ever needed you to trust me, now is the time."

Shayla cried softly as Lorenzo kissed her on the cheek. A second later he was gone.

"You gonna be okay?" Michelle slid behind the wheel.

Shayla nodded.

"Men can be so stupid at times. And I'm talking about Travis and Lorenzo."

"I don't care about him," Shayla mumbled.

"Yes you do." Michelle smiled. "Which is why I feel you'll go along with this idea I have."

Shayla stared at Michelle. "What idea?"

"Lemme use your phone for a second." she grinned. "I let Travis take mine."

***

"What's the plan?" Lorenzo broke the silence with Travis. "We can't follow La'Ashia forever, let alone in a stolen car."

Travis sped up on the highway to pass a dark sedan while keeping La'Ashia's tail lights in sight. "I'll figure out something."

Lorenzo looked at the fuel gauge. "Well, at least we have a full tank."

Travis nodded. "Tell me something. If you wouldn't have gotten jacked by Mikki, what were you planning to do with my bread?"

"Why do we even need to bring that up?"

"Because I want to know!" Travis lost control of his temper for a second. "All I did was try to put you on and you do this fucked up shit."

"Look man. I know I done fucked up but what's done is done. I... let's just drop it, okay. My issue right now is staying out of jail and—"

"We gonna have to handle La'Ashia," Travis said in a low tone. "I don't know how the hell she knows about Goldsboro, do you?"

"Nah. Maybe Derrick told her?"

Travis didn't respond. "Was the pussy good?"

"Huh?"

"Mikki or whatever the fuck her name is. Was the pussy worth it all?'

"Man, you're bugging."

"No I ain't. It's a simple damn question," Travis stated as he fought to keep his cool. It took all of his will not to steal off on Lorenzo. "It's kosher because the bitch was just a hoe anyway. I see you left out the parts of you fucking Mikki from Shayla."

Lorenzo refused to fall into a verbal conflict. "Yeah, and I plan to keep it that way."

Travis laughed. "Got it all figured out don't cha?"

"Nope. But I'm working on it."

Chapter Thirty-Five

Havelock, North Carolina
July 29th, Monday

A light rain greeted La'Ashia a few minutes past midnight when she reached the city limits of Havelock. La'Ashia knew that her hours on the road hadn't been a waste of her time. Mikki had a crib in Havelock, just a few blocks down the road from Kahneko's apartment. The traffic was thin as La'Ashia drove up the Main Street with one hand on the wheel. A quick glance at her smartphone showed that she was only a quarter of a mile from Kahneko's phone signal. She knew the area, having visited Kahneko numerous times behind Travis and Derrick's back. Driving through a green light, she laid the smartphone on the charger plate, then reached for her purse on the passenger seat. As the wipers swiped across the windshield, she fished inside her purse for her gun. Keeping her eyes on the road ahead, she pulled out the black, metal frame, polymer grip .22 pistol. Lorenzo's Ruger was too big for what she had in mind. She liked the small compact .22 pistol. It forced her to handled her business UCAP, up close and personal. At a red light, she popped the clip out to make sure it was fully loaded with twelve rounds. With one in the chamber and surprise riding along with her, thirteen rounds were more than enough to face Mikki. Federal agent or not, La'Ashia was on a course to show Mikki who the real bitch was. When the light turned green, she drove with one hand on the wheel and the other gripping the .22.

***

"Why are you stopping?" Lorenzo sat up when Travis suddenly slowed the late model Chevy Malibu in front of a closed hardware store. "La'Ashia kept going," Lorenzo added.

Travis stared straight ahead while the windshield wipers squeaked back and forth.

"Your plan worked," Travis admitted. "Why else would La'Ashia up and haul ass to Havelock? Mikki lives here, so she still has Kahneko's phone."

"Okay, that's true. But why are we pulled over?" Lorenzo asked as the rain drummed the roof of the car.

Travis sat back in the seat with both hands on the wheel. He closed his eyes. "I got a bad feeling about this."

"About what? You just said the plan worked. All we, I mean, all you gotta do now is catch Mikki and La'Ashia off guard. I know they are both strapped and well, that right there might be a big problem."

Travis sighed and turned to look at Lorenzo. "It ain't that."

"Well, what is it? What, we out of gas or something?"

Travis nodded at Michelle's smartphone on the dash. "Look at the screen."

Lorenzo viewed the screen for a few seconds. "Oh shit! Are you saying—"

211

"Yeah. And I don't believe in this being a coincidence."

"So what do we do now?"

Travis stared through the rain coated sunroof for a second. "We gotta be extra careful, because right now I don't know what the fuck is going on."

***

Mikki sunk her nails deep into Scott's back as he finished off rough and fast between her parted legs. Sweat covered them both inside the dim-lit bedroom.

"Stay inside me." Mikki licked his ear and raked her nails up his pale ass under the sheets.

"That was amazing!" Scott panted.

Mikki smiled up at him. "You were okay."

"You can't hurt my ego," he said stroking the slick curve of her left breast. "Not after the way your body responded to me."

"Okay, it was good. But don't go falling in love with me," she teased.

Scott and Mikki were forced to team up now. After the shoot-out, Mikki had ran nonstop for three blocks until Scott drove up behind her in Travis' XTS.

"Get in!" Scott had shouted. "We need each other and you know it. We can sort out our issues at a later time."

Mikki had no other choice but to trust Scott. Along their trip, she had held him at gunpoint for nearly ten minutes. He got right to the point and explained his reason for picking her up. He needed the money. The sex was just a needed form of letting some stress off.

"Are you sure no one in the bureau knows about this place?" Scott asked for the second time.

"We're safe here. Trust me." She met his gaze without blinking.

Scott rolled from between her legs then stared up at the ceiling. "Why did you let that bastard call the bureau?"

"He had a phone. I told you."

"Shit!"

"Where is your phone?" Mikki turned to her side to face him.

"It's gone. What about yours?"

"The same."

"Well, we both know how the bureau will come for us so we shouldn't have too much of a problem."

"Maybe we can like, stay together." Mikki reached under the sheets and softly formed a grip around Scott's dick.

"Mmm." He smiled at her. "That feels good, but staying together is a bad idea."

"Okay, what's a good idea?"

"Well, considering our messed up lives, I say we split the money you have and we go our separate ways. You know the ramifications if either of us is apprehended. I don't need to speak on that do I?"

Mikki shook her head then followed it with a smile. "Maybe they'll stop looking for us and—"

"No," Scott said, reading her mind. "We can never let our guard down. Not today, not tomorrow, not next week, not next month, not next—"

"Hey, hey, I get it." Mikki pressed her breast against his arm. "I'm glad you stopped and picked me up."

Scott chuckled. "I had to pass up on that clear shot I had."

"Mmm, I guess my ass looked too sweet to ruin huh?"

"I plead the fifth."

Mikki squeezed his new erection then snuggled her naked body even closer to him. "You've been wanting to have sex with me ever since we first met. Am I right?"

Scott nodded as Mikki's fingers teased his sac between his legs. "How do you do it?"

"Do what?"

"Sex. How do you do it so freaky with your undercover work?"

Mikki shrugged. "Would I be too common to say it's just business?"

"No. But what about now, with me?" He came up on his elbows.

"Does it matter? We both wanted to do it, right?"

"Absolutely, on your last statement. And if you keep stroking me like that I'll want to do it again."

"That's the idea." Mikki sat up and slid the sheets down to his knees. "I must be honest. I'm surprised by that." She smiled and nodded at his pink erection.

Scott roamed his gaze down her large breasts as she curled her fingers back around his smooth flesh. Closing his eyes, he released a soft moan then fell back to the pillow. A breath later, he felt her weight shifting on the bed. Just as he opened his eyes he was met with a face full of Mikki's freshly fucked pussy. For now, he turned his attention to returning Mikki's oral acts by tasting what she boldly offered. Business would be handled later.

***

La'Ashia muttered curses when her left foot landed in a puddle of mud. She lifted her foot slowly while balancing herself against the back wall outside of Mikki's home. The pouring rain soaked La'Ashia from her head to her now muddy feet. Moving at a slow crouch, she edged along the wall, drawing closer to the only lit bedroom window. She adjusted her eyes in the dark to make sure her next steps wouldn't send her on her ass. Step by slogging step, she kept a firm handed grip on the .22.

When she finally stopped, the bedroom window was inches above her. Taking a few breaths to calm herself, she slowly came up out of her crouch. "Fucking rain!" she mumbled. At her full height of only 5 feet 4 inches, she could barely see over the window pane and into Mikki's bedroom. Turning her head to the side, she peeked through a slit in the dark colored curtains. *Got your ass now!* La'Ashia could clearly see Mikki on the bed doing a 69 with a white man. *I gotta catch this bitch while she has a dick down her throat.* La'Ashia had an idea. She just hoped it wouldn't end up getting her killed or worse, in her view, thrown in prison for murder.

***

Mikki had the unwavering mindset of a black widow as she feverishly slid her lips up and down Scott's curved erection. She had no intentions of giving him one penny, nor letting him live a single minute after she was done fucking him. Her hips moved instinctively, pressing her drenched center against his twisting tongue and probing fingers. Using both hands, she gripped his solid base, slurping loudly. His moans were muffled between her legs that she clamped over his face.

Scott was caught up in the talented pleasure from Mikki's mouth. He assumed he was the one in control. Thinking she was trying to win him over through sex, he went along with it. He palmed her ass with both hands and flicked his tongue between her sapid folds then caught her off guard by smacking her on her hip. He later showed his control by forcing her to stop. Without words, he turned her around and made her sit down on his throbbing erection.

"Yesss!" Mikki threw her head back and promptly rocked her back against Scott with him firmly inside her. Her breasts bounced wildly as she twirled and bucked above him.

Scott fucked her back, repeating her name over and over. This time, it was longer than the first. Mikki later bit the pillow as Scott rammed the blunt head of his dick in and out of her pussy doggy-style. He wanted to dominate her. Baring his teeth, he fisted his hand in her hair while squeezing her rippling ass with the other. When she started to whimper, he knew her tough persona was broken. Closing his eyes, he pounded hard and long, caught up.

Mikki never missed a beat as she took all of Scott. Her body shuddered at one point when his strokes touched her tingly walls. Their flesh clapped in a steady beat, mixed with their moans and heavy breaths. Through it all, Mikki was on course. Inch by inch she slid her right hand under the pillow. Scott's dick had her toes curling but she shoved the pleasure aside and moved her hand even further.

"Yess! Ohh god! Scott!" She now had her hand at the head of the mattress. Looking over her shoulder, she took the chance to feel around for the butcher knife. Scott had his eyes shut, rocking in and out of Mikki's wetness. He wasn't gentle with her. His strokes were rushed and steady. His eyes popped open when Mikki's fingers tickled his swinging sac. Releasing her hair he filled his palms with her soft ass, finally slowing his pace. Mikki hugged the pillow with both hands hidden from Scott.

"Cum all over me." Scott breathed with his focus on his bare penetration.

"Keep fucking me!" Mikki replied. "Yess, don't stop."

"I won't stop until you cum all over my dick. Now do it." Scott squeezed her ass as he fought to keep his control inside Mikki. Reaching under her he started caressing her left breast. "Cum with me."

Mikki nodded, then twerked her pussy back against his forward push. Minutes later, she asked him to change positions. "I want to see your face when you cum."

Scott forced himself to slow to a stop and pull out. Sweat covered his forehead as he backed out of Mikki's sopping wet hole. Before he could ask how she wanted him, Mikki had turned around and put his dick back inside of her mouth. She slowly moved her lips down to his thick base then back up to his tip. She twirled her tongue around it five quick times while Scott remained up on his knees. Scott allowed Mikki to have her way with him. Her tongue sent chills up and down his arms. She nibbled along the length of him while lightly rubbing his balls. He felt safe since her weapon was laid on the dresser across the room. Moments later, he was back under Mikki as she wildly rode him. The headboard thumped against the wall, adding to the steady sounds of their moans and skin against skin slapping.

Scott guided Mikki up and down with a firm grip on her waist. "I'm cumming!" he grunted.

Mikki stared down at Scott with both hands on his chest. She tighten her pussy and rode him nice and easy. Her eyes never left his face. She waited, riding him to a strong climax. When his grip dug into her sweaty flesh and his body became stiff, she eased her right hand off his chest. Scott's climax came in a blur. He closed his eyes, his mouth fell open, forming an O. Mikki felt Scott's climax spurting inside of her even as she gripped the wooden handle of the 7-inch long butcher knife. She sat up with the knife, suppressing a moan but fully willing to commit her next act. When Scott opened his eyes, Mikki was in mid swing with the knife. His arms came up a split second after the razor edge of the knife sliced open his throat. His final fight left him with enough strength to twist Mikki off. She simply slid off the bed and stared at Scott trying to stem the heavy flow of blood flowing from his neck.

"Should of never let your guard down." Mikki shook her head then tossed the bloody knife on the bed. "And you should have shot me when you had the chance."

A minute later Scott was no longer a problem for Mikki. Leaving his body on the bed, she crossed the bedroom and went into the shower. Her face was expressionless when she stopped in front of the mirror. Fucking Scott wasn't going to place any regrets on her shoulders. Like most men, she knew Scott would let his guard down when it came to a fresh pussy and a pretty face. In the shower, she allowed the hot water to wash the spots of blood off her breast and stomach. It spiraled down the drain, close to the balance of Mikki's fucked up life. She showered quickly, with all thoughts on what her next move would be. Above all, she would be leaving Havelock and the state of North Carolina at the soonest. Lay low for a week or two, obtain a new fake I. D. and then she could be on her way out of the country will *all* of her money. As she wrapped a towel around her wet body she looked around the bathroom one last time. So many memories flooded her mind. Grinning and shaking her head she thought of the last time she and Derrick had fucked in the shower. Turning from the sink she opened the door and came face to face with a surprise visitor that left her speechless. The gun in her face stopped her from all thoughts of spending a single penny on the run.

Chapter Thirty-Six

"Step on out with your hands up, bitch!" La'Ashia ordered Mikki with the .22 pointed at her face. "And don't even think about doing nothing stupid. You already know why I'm here and what I want, so let's get down to it. Where the loot?"

"It's not here."

La'Ashia lowered the .22 then pulled the trigger.

"Aaaarrghh!" Mikki howled in pain as she crumpled to the floor. Her training kicked in as she rolled to her side with blood pooling from the hole in her left thigh. Clenching her teeth she yanked the towel off then balled it up to cover the wound.

"Wrong answer, hoe!" La'Ashia stood over Mikki with the .22 now aimed at her face. "I have twelve more to pop your dumb ass with so come off it!"

Mikki grimaced as the pain throbbed. Laid out on her back, she struggled to control her breathing. "Fuck you!" Mikki gasped. "Ain't telling you shit."

"Oh yes you will." La'Ashia nodded. "Now I'll give you three options. I can pop you in your left foot... or your right... or you can tell me where the money is. One, two, or three?"

"I'm a federal agent!" Mikki screamed.

"So," La'Ashia shrugged. "That badge ain't gonna help your ass tonight, now is it?"

"Go to hell!"

"Not before I leave with the money. Now holler back at me. One, two, or three. You got ten seconds. Ten, nine, eight, seven—"

"Do it, bitch!"

"Six, five, four, three… two—"

"Say another number and that one will be your last!"

La'Ashia's stomach knotted when she heard Travis' voice behind her.

"Drop your gun!" Travis pressed the steel handle of the wrench against the back of La'Ashia's head.

The instant La'Ashia dropped the .22, Lorenzo snatched it up. When La'Ashia turned toward Travis, she saw the wrench and realized she'd been tricked.

"Surprised to see me?" Travis shoved La'Ashia and got up in her face. "Bitch, where my mutha fucking bread?"

"You need to ask your grimy ass bitch!" She stood her ground showing she wasn't scared.

"Look who's talking," Travis sneered. "And FYI, bitch! I knew about your little stickup hustle you had going on with Kahneko."

Lorenzo had backed up near the door, so he could cover the entire bedroom with the .22.

"I need help," Mikki moaned on the floor.

Travis stepped around La'Ashia and stared at Scott's body on the bed. "You fucking him, too?" Travis asked Mikki. "Nevermind, it doesn't matter. Where my shit at?"

Mikki shook her head. "Help... me first." The loss of blood had made her weak. Using all the strength she had, she kept pressure on the wound.

"Bitch, you must think I'm playing!" Travis turned toward Lorenzo. "Lemme see that gun for a second."

"Nah, I got it."

Travis clenched his jaw. This was a battle he couldn't win right now. "Whatcha mean, 'nah?' What the fuck?"

"Yo, let's get what we came for and get the fuck outta here." Lorenzo reminded Travis.

Travis nodded. "Yeah, you got it," he said through clinched teeth. *Fuck he talking about we!*

Lorenzo turned his attention to La'Ashia as Travis turned and knelt on one knee next to Mikki. He assumed she was telling Travis about the money as she whispered in his ear. "Why did you kill Kahneko?" Lorenzo asked La'Ashia.

She smacked her lips. "Right now you need to worry about your own life and how the fuck you getting out of here alive."

***

"Baby you have to trust... me," Mikki spoke in a low tone, so her words didn't reach Lorenzo.

"Trust you! You done fucked my man, stole my—"

"Please listen. I can make it up to you. Lorenzo… he hasn't been truthful with you, baby. I told you I could get your money back… and I did—"

"Yeah, for your gotdamn self. Bitch, I'm not stupid!"

"Travis, please. There is so much that you don't know about. I was going to call you and tell you everything and give your money back. I… was always loyal to you."

Travis sighed. "You couldn't see loyal even if it was tatted on your forehead."

Mikki closed her eyes as her mind fought for a way out. Opening her eyes she looked up at Travis. She saw hate, but she had to go forward with her last hope. "Baby, let me prove myself to you."

"How? This I gotta hear."

She cleared her throat. "Don't trust Lorenzo. The second you have the money you're dead… including me. Over… on my dresser is your gun that Scott took from you. I had to do all this to get your money back."

"Well, what about all that fly shit you were popping off when I called you?"

Mikki winced as a sharp pain nearly forced her to blackout. "It… was all for show. I swear to you, baby."

"Where's my fucking money?" Travis said through his teeth. "Tell me, or bleed to death!"

"911. What's the nature of your call?"

"Um, I live on Shipman Road in Havelock and I think I heard a gunshot a few minutes ago."

"Where?"

"At my neighbor's home. I also think I saw someone creeping in the backyard. It might be a robbery or—"

"Ma'am what's the address, please?"

"Oh right. It's um...725 Shipman Road."

"Thank you and I'm sending officers now. And what is your address?"

"723 Shipman Road."

"Okay, can you stay on the line and keep me updated on everything until the police arrive?"

"Uh, I guess so. I can see clearly through my bedroom window and... I'll keep my lights turned off."

***

"What did she say?" Lorenzo asked Travis as he crossed the bedroom toward the dresser.

"Let me handle this! Just keep an eye on La'Ashia. He saw three guns—his, Scott's and Mikki's.

"What are you looking for?" Lorenzo asked.

Travis pretended to search for something in one of the drawers. Stealing a quick glance up in the mirror, he saw Lorenzo still near the door. "My car keys."

"Man, we need to hurry the fuck up," Lorenzo stressed.

"Chill, Zo." Travis turned around. "This here is my beef. It was my bread that was stolen. So you can dead all that *we* shit. I'm not walking up outta here without my bread. You want to bounce, the door is right behind you."

"What about La'Ashia?" Lorenzo asked as he glanced at Mikki. *Fuck that bitch!*

Travis shrugged. "Kill the slut. We can't let her walk. Not after she made that comment about Goldsboro."

"Ain't no snitch!" La'Ashia defended herself from across the room. "You're the clown that was making deals with the Feds."

"Bitch, ain't nobody talking to you!" Travis glared at La'Ashia. "From what I was told, you got a body hanging over your head as it is."

"You weren't there—"

"It doesn't matter!" Travis shouted. "So what's up, Lorenzo? You gonna straighten your face and finally put in some work for PBH?"

"PBH is over," Lorenzo replied.

"Is that what you think? Scott is out of the game and Mikki will soon follow. As for Sergeant Parker and Mac, they can get it, too. You got the gun... I don't." Travis nodded at La'Ashia. "What's the problem?"

Lorenzo sighed as he weighed his options. He couldn't trust La'Ashia to stay silent about Goldsboro. With a murder charge hanging over her head, he doubted she would stick to the code of the streets.

"So it's true," Travis concealed his move from Lorenzo. "You called the police back in Goldsboro."

"What?"

Travis nodded. "While you were in the bathroom. You called the police just so we wouldn't kill that bitch!"

Lorenzo lowered the gun from La'Ashia to his side. Travis reacted quickly and leveled the terms with two guns.

"Move an inch and it's over for your ass!" Travis stared at Lorenzo as La'Ashia backed up against the wall. "Drop the gun!"

"Man, what the fuck!" Lorenzo snarled.

"Should have left me in the trunk, nigga! What, you think I'ma forgive and forget all the grimy shit you did to me? Your broke ass was down and out and I gave you a full plate to eat off of. And what thanks do I get in return? You fuck my bitch and hit my stash. Ain't no making up from that. Not in my book!"

"It doesn't have to go down like this." Lorenzo flexed his grip on the .22.

"I don't give a fuck how it goes down! But I can tell you one thing, it ends tonight. Right here, right fucking now."

"Travis," Mikki moaned from the floor. "Just—"

"Oh shit!" La'Ashia backed up from the window. "We've got company!"

A second later the flashing strobe lights atop two Havelock police cars could be seen through the curtains.

Lorenzo took one glance then hauled ass for his escape out the back door. La'Ashia did the same, taking a chance of being shot in the back. Travis dropped one of the guns and ran over to Mikki.

"Where is it!" Travis shoved the barrel under her chin. "You got five seconds."

Mikki closed her eyes. She couldn't face her problems. If left alive she knew she would go down hard for Scott's murder. And even if she told Travis where the money was he would still kill her. Opening her eyes she spat in his face. "Fuck you! And by the way, I fucked your cousin Derrick!" Mikki waited for the gun to go off.

***

Police sirens grew louder as Lorenzo and La'Ashia left the scene behind. They ran at full speed through back yards without looking back. At one point they reached a high wooden fence that La'Ashia couldn't climb over. As she struggled to get over the top she was caught off guard when Lorenzo gave her a needed boost. The rain continued to come down as they ran under a swing set.

"Where is your car?" Lorenzo asked out of breath as he leaned up against a tree.

La'Ashia had a scared look on her face as she shook her head. "Too close to the scene. That place is gonna be crawling with cops. We can't go back."

"Fuck!" Lorenzo looked up at the moon. "C'mon, we gotta keep moving before they put the dogs on our trail."

***

Travis had seen the hopeless look in Mikki's eyes. She wanted him to pull the trigger. With less than a minute to spare, he searched the closet and found his money at his feet. Mikki screamed at his back as he ran out of the bedroom, forcing her to deal with her fucked up situation. Rushing out the back door into the rain, he made his narrow escape just as the police knocked on the front door. Seeing no signs of Lorenzo or La'Ashia, he hurried off toward a low fence and crossed the grass.

***

"I'm not walking through that yucky ditch!" La'Ashia backed up. "What if it's filled with snakes or shit like that?"

"We have to. It'll throw the dogs off." Lorenzo was down on one knee trying to catch his breath. "We can't run forever and you can hear the dogs."

La'Ashia shivered as a breeze chilled her arms and face. "Why did you run into the woods? I can't see a damn thing," she complained.

"We're on the run okay? You wanna run along the street, go ahead."

"Why are you helping me?"

Lorenzo looked over his shoulder at her. She was soaked head to toe. "Why didn't you pull the trigger on me back in Clayton?"

La'Ashia shrugged. "I don't know," she muttered. "I don't know about shit right now!"

"Look, we have to walk through this ditch. It ain't deep and—"

"I can't," La'Ashia whined. She wasn't tough for this.

Lorenzo stood. "Get on my back. I'll carry you."

"There's a motel not far from here. If you think this can get the dogs off us, we can get a room until things calm down. I… we can catch a cab back to my car tomorrow and—"

"One thing at a time. Let's get to that motel and get the hell out of this rain."

***

Thirty minutes later, Lorenzo and La'Ashia were safe and warm inside the seedy motel. Lorenzo sat at the foot of the bed with the lights off while La'Ashia sat on the floor.

"Why did you help me over that fence?" La'Ashia asked after she finally caught her breath.

"It was just a reaction, I guess."

"You're not like Travis or Derrick."

"How am I different?" Lorenzo asked impassively with his head down.

"You care about people. Even after they did you dirty."

"And look where it has gotten me."

La'Ashia coughed. "I need to get out of these wet clothes before I catch a cold."

"Me too." Lorenzo stood. "And shower."

"Um, you can go first," La'Ashia suggested. "And don't use all the hot water."

"Ladies first." Lorenzo pointed toward the bathroom.

La'Ashia fingered her wet hair off her face. "I really don't trust you like that, so you can go in front of me."

Lorenzo yawned. "Either way, one of us will be out here while the other is in the shower."

"That's what I'm trying to get you to see."

"This is stupid."

"We have another choice."

"What, we don't take a shower at all?"

La'Ashia untied her wet shoes. "No. I was thinking maybe we could just take a shower together.

Chapter Thirty-Seven

Havelock, North Carolina

July 29th Monday

"Wake up! It's on the news!" La'Ashia shoved Lorenzo then raised the volume on the TV.

Lorenzo rolled over, yawned then sat up next to La'Ashia rubbing his eyes. "What are they—"

"Shhh." She held up her hand. "I don't know. I just turned on the TV."

Lorenzo looked at the screen as a dark haired female reporter stood in front of Mikki's house. In the lower left portion of the TV, *Live 9:22am* was highlighted in a bold white font.

> *...arrived last night at the home you see behind me, here on Shipman Road in Havelock. At this point, we know two people were found deceased inside, but local authorities are being tight lipped with any further details. And not too long ago a new development occurred by the arrival of four FBI agents from Raleigh. No suspects are in custody and the crime scene is being handled, unlike anything I've ever seen before. Again, if you're just now tuning in, two—*

"Travis must've killed Mikki." Lorenzo slid off the bed and treated La'Ashia to another sight of his nakedness.

"Looks that way," La'Ashia replied as she sat cross-legged on her side of the bed. "I don't think the police are looking for us." She turned from the TV and couldn't stop the urge to ogle between Lorenzo's legs. *I can't believe we fucked last night.*

"We need to find out what's up with Travis." Lorenzo searched for his boxers until he found them on the floor.

"Why?" She frowned.

"What if he didn't get the money? And what if—"

"Fuck Travis and that money. Look at all the crazy bullshit we've been through. One day I got a gun in your face and the next I'm all up on your dick like a hooker."

"Uh, about last night." Lorenzo slid his boxers up as La'Ashia made no effort to cover her breasts.

"What about it?" she asked uncertainly. "We were both highly strung out on our emotions and well... fucking was a good way to let some stress off. Was it good to you?"

Lorenzo turned and searched for his socks. Of course it was good, better than good. He knew she wanted to do something the moment she suggested that they take a shower together. Again he was weak when it came to making a choice between having sex with La'Ashia or not.

"If it makes you feel better. " La'Ashia slid off the bed. "I kinda regret doing what we did last night."

"Let's just focus on getting up outta here. What happened here, stays here."

La'Ashia crossed the room and came up behind Lorenzo. "I can deal with that. Can you?" She slid her hands up his back. To her surprise, he stiffened.

"You need to get some clothes on," Lorenzo scolded as he caught her in his sideview.

"Do you have a plan or something?" she asked hiding her slight surprise of rejection. "If you do, you're on your own. Like I said before, I'm done with this mess."

Lorenzo turned around and willed himself to ignore La'Ashia's tempting nakedness. His dick was on its own route. "Aren't you worried about looking over your shoulder for Travis and Derrick?"

"Please." La'Ashia rolled her eyes. "Just because I have a pussy don't mean I'm pussy. I got guns too, and I ain't afraid to let'em bust." She smiled, cocking her head. "Why do you ask? Are You starting to care about me after I let you up in this good ole million? Nah, I'm just trippin', Lorenzo." She giggled. *Damn! I wish we could do it again. Oh well.*

"Can I tell you something?"

La'Ashia nodded.

"You're one crazy ass—"

"Bitch." She laughed then boldly reached down to rub his semi-hard wood. "And I'll tell you something. That dick was OMG last night, baby."

As bad as he wanted to dig La'Ashia out again, his needs won out. He needed to reach Travis and find out what was going on.

***

Minutes later, Lorenzo paced the room with La'Ashia's smartphone. With La'Ashia in the shower, he took the chance to call Shayla. "Pick up, baby," he murmured while thinking of a good explanation for calling from La'Ashia's phone. How about the truth? No, he couldn't do that. Well, at least not the full truth. Just as he started to end the call it was answered. He swiped his fingertip across the speakerphone icon.

***

"Shayla! Baby, I—"

"Shayla can't come to the phone right now."

Lorenzo paused in his tracks. "Travis, put Shayla on the phone!"

"Can't," Travis disobeyed. "She's um, tied up right now. And I mean that in a true sense."

Lorenzo took a deep breath then sat at the foot of the bed. "Man, stop playing and put Shayla on the phone."

"Playing? Bruh, I stopped playing games a long time ago. Yeah, I see you're still with La'Ashia because I know you didn't merk her ass and—"

"Put Shayla on the phone gotdammit!"

"What part of she's tied up do you not understand? I'll break it down for ya. I got your pretty little bitch tied up. It took a little fight, but she's no more trouble for me. Now listen up. You owe me and PBH big time, so—"

"She's innocent, Travis! If you got beef, it's with me, not her!"

"Ain't no if to it! You know we got beef! FYI, yeah I got my mutha fuckin' bread back and like I just said, you owe me!"

Lorenzo squeezed his eyes shut as a dread of hopelessness came over him. "Travis," he pleaded. "Please don't hurt her."

"I won't, but if you don't handle something for me you can visit her at the morgue."

"C'mon, man. Why it gotta be like this?" Lorenzo squeezed the phone.

"You broke the code, my trust, so it's no love for you, bruh. I let you under my roof, dawg! You cut off now... ain't no love."

"W-what do you want?" Lorenzo had his mind made up that he would do anything to save Shayla.

"Your life, muthafucka! But right now that ain't helping me none. So, here's what you'll do for me. The true source of my problem is Sergeant Parker. Once she finds out about Scott she'll just run her mouth about PBH to the next Fed. Go see the bitch and put in work and you know what the fuck I'm talking about. You got twenty-four hours to have that bitch obituary material."

"I'll do it, man, I swear. Just let me talk to Shayla, please."

"Yo, I told her all about your little affairs with Mikki and Kahneko." Travis ignored Lorenzo's request. "She wasn't too happy about that."

"Please, man."

"Hold on. Don't want your bitch ass to start crying and shit."

Lorenzo felt a vise closing in on his world as he waited to hear Shayla's voice. He realized now that money was the cause of his downfall. His greed, his thirst for that quick and easy hustle was now a pill of regret.

"I changed my mind," Travis said a few seconds later. "I'll text you a picture of her so—"

"No! I need to... know that she's alive. Please don't—"

"Nigga, don't push your gotdamn luck! Look, um, it's almost ten o'clock and that bullshit Maury is on. I'll take her picture in front of the TV and that's all your ass is getting so there it is."

239

Lorenzo sighed and held back his threats toward Travis. He had to stay in control for the sake of Shayla. "How can I get Shayla back after I do this?"

"I haven't thought about that just yet. Right now you need to be getting on over to paying Sergeant Parker a visit. And I want proof too! Matter of fact, cut that snitching ass bitch tongue off after you pop her. Play games with me or go to the police and I'll make Shayla suffer!"

Lorenzo closed his eyes, flushing out a single tear.

"Clock is running, bruh. I suggest you do what it do and get things popping. Now be a good boy and put in some work for PBH. Don't call me until that bitch is the owner of a toe tag!"

The connection ended before Lorenzo could get in another word. He mentally sunk into a thick mood of despair that shook his meaning of life. For Shayla, he would risk his freedom and life without falter or thought. As he forced his mind to cling to any hope of coming out on top, La'Ashia walked silently and laid her hand on his shoulder.

"I have to—"

"I heard everything," La'Ashia cut him off. "Do you think he's for real?"

Lorenzo fought to gather himself to speak without falling apart. He would never forgive himself if any harm came to Shayla. Several seconds moved between them before Lorenzo was able to speak. "I can't take that risk to call his bluff. I have to do it."

La'Ashia shook her head. "There has to be another way. You already saw how Travis gets down for PBH. Look at how he told Derrick to kill them other dudes that fucked up. The way I see it, Travis can kill two birds with one stone. What if he is setting you up to go down for this hit? Think about it."

"Ain't shit to think about." Lorenzo stood. "I'll do whatever it takes."

"I understand all that. But speed balling and being stupid shouldn't be one of them. Now if you'll gimme a few minutes, I have an idea."

Lorenzo had to stand and face his dilemma. His next move, his next choice would test the balance on Shayla living to see the next day or not.

***

"So many secrets between all of us." Travis lifted Shayla's chin. "Derrick told me about that porno-style lap dance you gave him at the strip joint. Does Lorenzo know about that? See, if you wanted money you could have come to me. You know I always liked you."

"Then… why are you doing this to me?" Shayla sobbed.

Shayla jerked back from his unwanted touch then strained at the thick duct tape that held her strapped to the chair. "Don't touch me!"

Travis laughed humorlessly. "You better be glad I have a line I won't cross."

Shayla turned from his leery stare.

"Are you gonna tell me how you popped up in Havelock last night?"

"I followed you," she told half of the truth. She had in fact followed Michelle's smartphone signal. Her concern was for Lorenzo but she ended up picking up Travis. He had lied and said Lorenzo was right behind him until Shayla became suspicious and started asking too many questions. Shayla could still see the fear in Michelle's eyes when Travis pressed a gun to her head. He had forced Michelle to drive to Kinston while Shayla cried silently in the passenger seat.

The small bedroom she was in was lit by a single lamp in the corner. The bed was unmade and the room itself, junky. Shayla saw no means of escape from the sturdy chair or the house. Thick black blankets were nailed over the two windows behind Shayla. She was lost on the time as each second seemed like an hour.

Travis stood. "At least you're being treated better than Michelle."

Shayla ignored him.

"Her having a kid by me don't mean shit. Do you know about her fucking Derrick? Bitch ain't shit but a cheap priced slut. Ain't mad, ain't no fun if my cuzzo can't have none.

242

Hell, knowing her ass, she's probably in the other room trying to suck or fuck her way up outta here."

Shayla remained silent, hoping Travis would leave. She filled her mind with thoughts of seeing her son again. Anything, she would do anything and give up any part of herself to make it back to her son.

***

"How your leg feeling?" Travis asked Derrick in the tiny living room.

Derrick laid his crutches on the sofa then gingerly sat down. "I'm good. Just a little sore."

Travis walked over to the front door and took a peek outside. A semi-automatic AK-47 filled his hand.

"Do you know what the fuck you're doing, fam?" Derrick asked from the sofa. "First, you sit at the table and eat with a Fed, and now you got these two bitches tied up in the back. Okay, you said Scott and Mikki are toast and you think that busta ass Lorenzo is gonna put in work on Parker."

"He will if he wanna see Shayla again."

Derrick adjusted his heavily bandaged leg. "What if he calls your bluff?"

Travis turned from the door. "Ain't bluffing, cuzzo." Travis stated. "Word on everything! I'll murder both them bitches if Lorenzo tries to play any fucking games with me!"

"Man this shit is crazy. And you're serious about Michelle?"

"Bitch don't mean shit to me. Do she mean anything to you?"

Derrick swallowed. "Hell no."

"Did Mikki or whatever the fuck her name was mean anything to you?"

"Why would she mean anything to me, fam? She was—"

"I once heard a person facing death would always tell the truth. You ever heard that before?"

"Man, you tripping. If you got something to—"

"Mikki told me about y'all two fucking. Is it true, cuzzo?"

Derrick averted his eyes to the floor. For the first time in his life, he had a reason to fear his flesh and blood. "Fam, I was spaced out on some—"

"It doesn't matter, cuzzo. Fuck these hoes. These hoes ain't loyal! That bitch took herself out, and I ain't missing her none. PBH is all I care about—"

"But the Feds—"

"They don't know shit! The investigation died with that cracker Scott. All we gotta do is take care of Parker and Lorenzo and we good. Everything can go back to like it was.

Derrick shook his head. "Shit, man I don't know 'bout all that."

244

"Well, that's the difference between you and me! I'm 'bout this life, cuzzo. I won't let this minor bullshit stop me from eatin'."

"You call this minor! PBH is being took down left and right! It's over, fam."

"Nah. Not for me."

"Really? So what's your plan now? You got everything figured the fuck out."

Travis glanced down at the AK-47. "I'ma pay Parker a visit and if Lorenzo don't show up… he'll regret it."

"And what about them?" Derrick nodded down the hall.

Travis stood with a far off look. "Kill 'em both then be ready to move when I get back."

Chapter Thirty-Eight

The sun retired behind a dark patch of clouds over Kinston a little after six p. m. Three blocks north of the PBH trap house La'Ashia and Lorenzo sat inside the Benz behind a broken-down school van.

"It makes sense." La'Ashia nodded at the GPS screen on the dashboard. "That's Travis' and Derrick's little hangout spot that they think I don't know about."

Lorenzo shifted anxiously in the seat. "How long Travis been gone?"

"Almost an hour."

Lorenzo sighed and ran his hand down his face. "I'm tired of just sitting here gotdammit!"

She couldn't argue with him. "You know he wouldn't leave your girl alone. And knowing what I do about Travis. He's fucking with somebody he can trust."

"Derrick," Lorenzo murmured as his hands turned into a fist. He stared straight ahead with hate and fear twisting his face.

"Could be," La'Ashia replied.

"What's the layout of the house?"

"Small. Two bedrooms I think."

"Backdoor?"

She shrugged. "Not sure. Never been inside."

Lorenzo couldn't waste another second with Shayla's life at risk. "Lemme hold your gun."

"Ok, but what if Travis pop back up?"

"I'll deal with that if it comes up."

"Maybe you should wait until—"

"No!" Lorenzo shouted. "Ain't waitin' for shit. I got to end this right now before it gets outta hand!" He stared at La'Ashia with his mind made up. Gun or no gun he was going to get Shayla back or die trying.

La'Ashia gave Lorenzo the Ruger .22. As he reached for the door she grabbed his arm. She wanted to help him even more. She quickly shared a plan, an idea that she thought would work. In truth, anything was better than the unplanned actions that Lorenzo had in mind.

Moments later he hurried up the sidewalk with the Ruger tucked away in his pocket. Glancing over his shoulder, he saw La'Ashia's face lit up from the glow of her smartphone. With limited options, he was cornered into trusting La'Ashia with Shayla's life and possibly his own life on the line.

**

Derrick paused the video game when a pair of headlights filled the small living room window. He struggled to his feet and up on one crutch with his Glock 30S. He winced as he hobbled over to the window to ease the cheap brown curtains open. By the sound of the raggedy engine, he knew it wasn't

Travis. Peering through a gap in the curtains he spotted an old beat-up, dark painted, Honda Accord station wagon.

"Ain't order no muthafuckin' pizza," he grumbled as a skinny teen hopped out of the Honda. He assumed the delivery was mixed up *again*. It was a norm with Hood Pizza and it's ghetto style management. Derrick carefully stuck the Glock in the front of his jeans the moved toward the door. He unlocked the three dead bolts with the rubber handle of the Glock exposed. As soon as he opened the door he could smell the coming rain. He stood in the doorway as the skinny black teen bopped up the wooden steps on the porch.

"Yo, you order a pizza?" the teen asked with his fitted cap turned backward.

Derrick frowned. "Nah."

"Man, shit!" The teen sucked his teeth. "Dis the third fucked up order in one day!"

"Ain't order no pizza, bruh. But if it's a non-pork pizza I'll buy it."

The teen thought it over and took a quick glance at the gun. He wasn't shook from the sight of it. "You're in luck, my man. I gotta hot large hamburger cheese pizza for eight bucks!"

Derrick nodded. "Yeah I'll get it. G'head and bring it in and sit it on the kitchen table."

The teen turned and stepped on the creaky step. At the last step, he turned back around and told Derrick he could get some breadsticks for an extra two bucks. Derrick added it to his order. He figured it would make sense to feed Shayla and Michelle. Leaving the door wide open, he turned and started down the hall to check on Shayla and Michelle. His progress was slow and painful on one crutch. When he neared the sofa, he heard the teen coming up behind him with the pizza. He could smell it.

"Wait in the kitchen and close the—"

In the next breath, Derrick was knocked hard to the floor. He fell flat and howled in pain when his leg banged against the edge of the living room table. The teen scrambled on Derrick's back. "Get the fuck off me!" Derrick elbowed the teen in his jaw then grimaced in pain as he tried to roll over. "Clumsy ass!" Derrick saw the pizza on the floor along with the breadsticks. "What the fuck wrong with you!"

The teen stood motionless against the wall. Wide-eyed he slowly lifted his arm and pointed over Derrick's head toward the door. "He… he pushed me."

Derrick rolled to his back and felt his stomach knot up at the sight of Lorenzo.

"Where's Shayla?" Lorenzo shouted with the .9-millimeter aimed at Derrick's face. He stood over him with his face tight. "G'head and reach for that gun so I can pop your fuckin' melon!"

Derrick shook his head. "Man, I…"

"Where is she!" Lorenzo shouted. "I swear to God I'll murder your bitch ass if you don't answer me!"

"Ch-chill man," Derrick stuttered lying flat on his back. "She in the back room."

Lorenzo reached down and snatched the .45 from Derrick's waist. Taking a step back, he quickly pocketed the .45.

"C'mon, Zo!" Derrick copped a plea. "We weren't gonna hurt—"

"Ain't got no rap for ya!" Lorenzo shouted. "You!" he called out to the teen. "Go and check the back rooms."

"Yo, fam. I didn't—"

"Go check the gotdamn rooms!" Lorenzo pointed his Ruger at the teen.

The teen winced and threw his hands up. "Okay, okay I'm going. Please don't kill me!" He sidestepped along the wall with his eyes locked on the daunting barrel pointed in his direction.

"Where Travis?" Lorenzo nudged Derick with his foot.

"I don't know!"

Lorenzo kicked Derrick in the ribs. "Quit lying! Keep fucking with me and I'ma have you on one leg?" Lorenzo pointed the .9 at Derrick's good kneecap.

"Wait, wait, wait! He went to see Sergeant Parker! I swear!" Derrick blurted the truth.

"For what?" Lorenzo shouted.

Before Derrick could answer, the teen yelled from the back. "Two girls back here!"

Lorenzo wanted to rush to the back, but he couldn't leave Derrick. "Get the fuck up!" He took a step back and kicked the second crutch across the floor toward Derrick. Just as the teen eased back into the living room they all heard someone running up on the porch. Lorenzo spun as the doorknob turned, gripping the .9 millimeter with an intent to murder. His mind was set. It was too late to turn back. He held the Ruger steady, aiming head high at the door. The footsteps had stopped. Silence. He waited. His finger tensed up on the trigger. The doorknob clicked and a second later La'Ashia eased inside. She paused when she saw Derrick.

Lorenzo sighed and lowered the gun. "What are you doing here?"

"You need to hurry your ass up!" She closed the door and shot a quick glance at the teen. It was her idea to order a pizza and have it sent to the trap spot. She intentionally ordered Derrick's favorite.

"Here!" Lorenzo handed Derrick's glock to La'Ashia. "Watch these two."

"Is your girl here?"

"Yeah."

La'Ashia thumbed the safety off the glock as Lorenzo rushed down the hall. She stared at Derrick as he stood up on the crutches. She read the hate in his eyes. "Thin line between love and hate, huh?"

He didn't say shit.

She shrugged. "Charge it to the game, baby."

***

Moments later, Travis slowed Shayla's Altima to a stop when he saw a car backing out of the trap. "Who the fuck?" he murmured, his eyes narrowed. He instantly knew something was fucked up when the car hauled ass up the street. No police in sight, nor did he hear any sirens. He snatched his new cell phone off the passenger seat and called Derrick. After eight unanswered rings, he ended the call. "Fuck!" he punched the top of the steering wheel. He thought first of his money and then his cousin. Everything he had worked for was a mere fifty yards up the street. He had a bad feeling as he sat inside the dark sedan. His hands gripped the steering wheel, his eyes never leaving the trap. A minute later he dialed Derrick's number again. Same result. No answer. He turned the car off then reached in the back for the AK-47. With the darkness as his ally, he hurried up the block with the AK concealed against his body. A dog barked across the street behind a chain-link fence as Travis neared the front gate of his trap spot. Just as he stepped from the sidewalk, La'Ashia appeared at the front door. Caught off guard by her presence he froze.

He blinked. She slammed the door. Travis snapped and raised the AK-47. He ran up to the house, flicking the safety off.

***

"Go, go, go! Leave out the back!" Lorenzo pushed Shayla behind him as he kept an eye on the front door.

"Lorenzo you don't—" She reached for his arm.

"Ain't got time to argue!" he turned as La'Ashia ran down the hall with Michelle. "You have to leave! I'ma slow this nigga down. Now trust me, baby. Go with La'Ashia, hurry!" Shayla was torn with emotions. She didn't want to leave Lorenzo behind. Tears fell from her eyes as she tore herself free and ran out the back door.

***

Seconds later Travis slid into the dark living room with the AK-47 up and ready. He eased the door shut with his elbow. "Derrick!" he shouted as he slowly scanned the living room.

"This shit is over Travis!"

Travis froze. "That you, Zo?" He aimed the AK down the hall. "You got that bitch La'Ashia back there too, huh?"

"Yeah. And I got Derrick, too!"

Travis eased toward the kitchen. "So we gotta work out a deal huh? Shit, how I even know he's still alive? Lemme hear his voice."

"I'm back in the—"

"Satisfied!" Lorenzo shouted from one of the bedrooms.

"Now how do we work this out, Zo?" Travis asked. "I'm telling you now, ain't dropping this AK for nothing! All I want is my money and cuzzo."

"And what do I get for it?"

"Your gotdamn life, nigga!"

"PBH is over Travis."

"Keep PBH outta your mouth!" Travis yelled. "Shit ain't over till I say it's over!"

"You fucked the hustle up when you started dealing behind our backs with the Feds. Did you share your little deal you had with the FBI with Derrick?"

"Shut the fuck up! Ain't up in here to talk to your bitch ass! I want my gotdamn bread! You nor that grimy bitch will step foot outta here with a dime of my shit!"

***

"How about we let the girls leave?" Lorenzo yelled as he stood behind Derrick with the .45 to his head.

"La'Ashia stays!" Travis replied.

"All or nothing!" Lorenzo kept the lie going to hold Travis up. "What's it gonna be?"

Derrick squeezed the rubber grips on the crutches. He had to do something before that bitch La'Ashia got away. There

254

was much more to be lost than the $531,600 that was initially stolen. Derrick knew beforehand that he would body Justin and the others that night in Goldsboro. He and Travis had planned ahead by tricking the other PBH members to bring all of their stashes to the trap on the same night they were murdered. Every bill was packed tight in three large duffle bags and every bill left with them bitches. Derrick *knew* he had to do something. He closed his eyes, took a deep breath, and yelled as loud as he could.

"Ain't nobody back here but me, cuzzo! Dem bitches gone wit' da bread! Aim high!' Derrick dropped to the floor as Lorenzo cursed.

***

Travis' heart missed a beat. Everything was slipping out of control. Stepping from the kitchen he blacked out and started busting with the AK-47. Wood chips and plaster blew off the wall as round after round punched through the thin wall. Brass shell casings jumped from the AK as the plastic stock kicked hard against Travis' shoulder. He kept firing, etching the wall while his ears rang with each shot.

***

Lorenzo cringed on the floor as bullets whizzed over his head. Dust and plaster fell all over him. Behind him and over by the bed he could hear Derrick screaming and seeking cover

255

under the bed. The TV exploded with a loud pop as a bullet smacked into the screen. The mirror on the dresser shattered and rained an avalanche of sharp shards to the floor. Lorenzo squeezed the .9 and forced his legs and arms to move under the shower of lead. When he reached the door, he stuck the Ruger blindly out into the hall and fired off two quick shots.

***

Travis tripped and tumbled over the table as he dove out of Lorenzo's line of fire. He landed hard on his shoulder and rolled up on one knee. "You ain't makin' it up outta here alive!" Travis fought to catch his breath as he scrambled behind the sofa. "I know where you rest your head at, Zo! Did You forget about that? I know where your bitch works at. And what about that daycare in Smithfield where your son goes to! What, you think I won't touch 'em? You started this! I can bounce right now and make your life a living hell! You listening to me, Zo?" He popped the clip out and saw it was half empty. "That sounds like your Ruger! What, you got a few rounds left. Well, I got fifteen, homie! Let's go to war gotdammit! Think you can rob me? Think PBH is soft? You ain't gonna do shit when I—"

A shot clapped and Travis winced. Before he could say anything he heard the window being broken. Rising to his feet, it suddenly dawned on him that Lorenzo was making his escape out the bedroom window. He eased around the sofa with the AK tucked under his chin. Slowly, he stepped over the pizza on the floor and stared down the hall.

"Derrick!" Travis shouted. "What's going on back there, cuzzo?"

He was met with silence. Inching along the hall, he flexed his grip on the wooden frame of the AK. His finger tensed on the trigger. Travis held his breath as he came to a stop just a few feet from the bedroom. The door was open. He waited, looking over the barrel. Another silent step put him closer. He faintly heard the sounds of the night coming in through the busted out bedroom window. Lorenzo was gone. Filled with a rage, he rushed inside the bedroom and met the unexpected. The AK slipped from his hands as a long mournful wail sailed through his lips. "Noooo!" He dropped to his knees, just inches from Derrick's lifeless body. He lowered his head, filled with a pain that he never knew. This was a part of the hustle that Travis never sought to face. He stared at the blood he knelt in. Derrick's blood.

"I'm... sorry, cuzzo," Travis cried with blood on his hands. "Damn!" His body shook with anger and revenge toward Lorenzo. "I'ma kill 'em all," he sobbed, meaning every promise. He would act tonight. He would pay Shayla's mom a visit and murder her on sight! Mother, son, father, friend, Travis would show no pity. The sudden sound of police sirens broke Travis from his daze. He had to leave. He would mourn his cousin later and forever. As he stood, Lorenzo eased out of the closet with the .45 cocked. All he heard, the last he heard, was the closet door creak. Lorenzo couldn't live in fear of his family having to face Travis. He couldn't reason with Travis anymore. There would be no beef being squashed. There would be no peace if Travis lived. Lorenzo fired the .45 at the back of Travis' head and ended PBH.

Chapter Thirty-Nine

Eight months later

The federal investigation on PBH reached a dead end, and no arrests were made. Agents Scott Wilson and Jacqueline D. Loh aka Mikki hadn't left any paper or digital trails behind for the FBI and state officials to follow. Every statement that Sergeant Parker had given Wilson was shredded or never filed to begin with.

Parker was alive and well with no idea how death had missed her. Having to work overtime had saved her from Travis' visit. With Travis and Agent Wilson dead, she kept quiet and maintained her secret relationship with Mac. The FBI knew nothing about her and she took it for what it was worth. With a divorce from her husband, her focus stayed firmly on Mac and the hustle behind bars didn't stop. As for Mac, he took it day by day and lived his life to the fullest behind bars. With Sergeant Parker in his pocket, and constantly facing his life in prison as his reality, he made the best of his hell.

Michelle was fully settled in her new home and career down in Miami, Florida, doing porn. She held no harsh feelings over Lorenzo taking Travis' life. When the time came, she would reluctantly lie to her son about Travis. In her view, he was never a part of her life, nor her son's, just a careless one-night stand. Through it all, she would keep her secret and live her life as if Travis never existed.

***

Lorenzo and Shayla were back on stable terms. He came clean with all of his mistakes and through time she forgave him. Killing Travis and Derrick wasn't something he was proud of, but for the sake of his family, it was just. Money wasn't a stress over his household any longer. With his name free of any connections to PBH and the murders, he settled back into a normal life. All that mattered to him was Shayla and his son. He held a small amount of guilt while living off the money he had taken from Travis. In trying to correct his wrongs toward PBH he realized it was a mistake. Travis had crossed the line when he pulled Shayla into the issue. It was the highest form of no remorse in the code of the streets.

He never knew how much money La'Ashia took from the trap house. It was enough for her to overlook the stash he took from Travis added with what she took from Derrick. Just to keep him off her back, she had given him twenty bands ($20,000) before she hit the road. He assured her that he wouldn't say shit about Kahneko's unsolved murder. The last he heard of La'Ashia was two months ago. She had opened a beauty salon down in Atlanta, Georgia, retiring from her life of taking men fast for that green. Speaking of retiring, Lorenzo was thankful that Shayla's stripping days were over with. Whatever future problems they should face, they would do it together as a family and not apart.

THE END

About the Author

Victor L. Martin is near the end of a nineteen-year bid in the DPS prison system in North Carolina. Pretty Boy Hustlerz is Victor's fourth title with WCP since his debut in 2010 with The Game of Deception. Victor was born in Richmond, VA and raised in Selma, North Carolina and Miami, Florida. Single with no kids allows Victor to place total focus on his career. In the summer of 2018, Victor will regain his freedom, after 19 long years. For more info on Victor L. Martin and his books, please visit his Facebook site by searching for Victor L Martin.

For phone interview request, please contact management at victorlmartin75@gmail.com

For direct contact, please visit his website for his current address.

Facebook – Twitter – Instagram (victorlmartin75)

CPSIA information can be obtained
at www.ICGtesting.com
Printed in the USA
LVHW01*1838280218
568196LV00014B/246/P

9 781947 732056